The Magician's Beautiful Assistant

The Magician's Beautiful Assistant

and Other Stories

Rachel Wyatt

Hedgerow Press
2005

National Library of Canada Cataloguing in Publication Data
Wyatt, Rachel, 1929-
The Magician's Beautiful Assistant and
other stories / Rachel Wyatt

ISBN 0-9736882-2-X

I. Title.
PS 8595.Y3M34 2005 C813'.54 C2005-905664-9

Published and distributed in Canada by
Hedgerow Press,
P.O. Box 2471,
Sidney, B.C. V8L 3Y3
hedgep@telus.net
www.hedgerowpress.com

"The Woman who Drowned in Lake Geneva" was first published in *The Malahat Review* (no. 141, 2002)

The cover art is a detail from the perforated painting *Darwin Star Steer Dance Third Night* by Pat Martin Bates, in the artist's collection.

Cover and text design: Frances Hunter
Cover photography: Robbyn Gordon

Printed and bound in Canada
by Morriss Printing, Victoria, B.C.

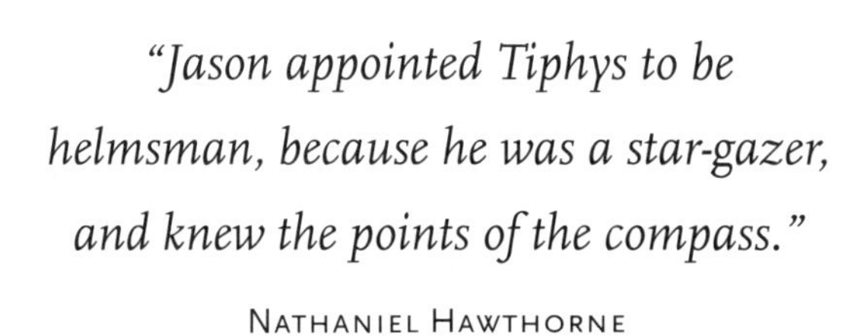

"Jason appointed Tiphys to be helmsman, because he was a star-gazer, and knew the points of the compass."

NATHANIEL HAWTHORNE

Contents

Goats

SOMEONE HAD BEEN TELLING THE TRUTH. Someone was sent for. In the upper room, the boss waited. Someone climbed two flights of stairs. The handwritten sign taped to the elevator door said, 'Not in use,' which could be interpreted two ways. At any rate someone climbed two flights to reach the boss's office.

"Do you see," the boss said, "what you've done?" He spoke in his kindest tone, like the sound of a rasp on metal.

Someone said, "It was the truth."

The foundations of the building shook.

Three board members entered the room.

A frown moved from face to face.

"The trickle-down effect," one said.

"There will be a deluge."

***

Bernard backed out of the room and ran down five flights of stairs to the underground garage and then remembered that the Ford was at the shop having its six-month check-up. On the bus he sat beside a woman who was telling a friend across the aisle that her night job in the department store was coming to an end and she was desperate. Bernard glanced at her. Her hair was thin and hung in strands about her face. Her teeth had been neglected. They wanted her to work Sundays too and she'd refused. Her companion at first had no comfort to offer but then said, "Your kids are great." "You're right," the desperate one replied, and became more cheerful. Bernard wanted to congratulate her on having fine kids and give her hope for a better life. He smiled at her as he made his way out of the bus. It was the best he could do.

The town, built in 1923, was planned by a left-handed architect so the streets were narrow. In his clever design, he hadn't considered the rights of the right-handed. He had though allowed for a rail up the steep steps to the sanctuary and made the access to the library wide. Four schoolchildren were able to walk up the steps side by side, holding hands. Bernard took note of it as he walked down the street to his house and wished that the calculations in his life were still simple.

★★★

Charity was beginning to dry up. Marion had been talking all afternoon and at four-thirty she stormed out of the room saying that unless her demands were met, she would strew the place with bodies or facsimiles thereof. Shrieks of laughter greeted the threat and there were very few offers of cash. People tried to touch her on the way out but she had learnt that it paid to move quickly. She ran past the TV cameraman who hung around outside the hotel waiting for something to happen: he had only to be patient and before long there would be a drug bust or at least a traffic accident.

★★★

Bernard began to tell about his dreadful day, the shocking figures, his meeting with the boss, the board, the probable outcome, but Marion countered with, "Tell me later. It's getting dark, becoming night. Put your other jacket on. We have to go out."

"That is the last thing," he said.

"My love," she said, and he changed.

A pity, Marion thought, that they had to mix with her colleagues. Several of them were standing near the buffet. They weren't eating but held onto their wine glasses tightly and glanced around the room as if searching for someone. She and Bernard left early.

★★★

It was too soon to watch out of the window. The children had promised to be back by eleven and that meant midnight. An arrangement understood by both parties. An ad in the journal offered for sale a brass telescope as used by Admiral Nelson. *Identical in every respect.* It was a bargain. Buy two and get the third one free. For people with three hands or for those who wanted to give unwieldy gifts to their loved ones for Christmas? *What do you think I am, a peeping Tom?* And there goes that relationship. The kids came in at one. What kind of time is this? Moon and stars and laughter but safe home at last. Let's not elaborate. Your father and I are exhausted. Mom, goodnight.

★★★

Someone had told the truth and the shares were sinking. They had chosen a culprit but were afraid to hang him out to dry too early. The company could only hold on and hope for an upswing. They prayed for a major tragedy that would keep their story off the front pages. Thank goodness it was Friday.

★★★

On Sunday before he'd had a chance to read the paper in peace, Bernard was mashing potatoes with a violence that was shaking the counter top. Marion had burnt the roast. Who cooks roasts these days? Can we afford beef? It could be infected. Should we be eating it at all?

Bernard said to his mother, "There will be changes." And she replied, "There always are," as if he'd reached the age of thirty-nine without knowing that. She thought of him as unaware and he resented it. He kissed her gladly when she left to go back to her apartment. She would spend the next few hours playing Patience on her computer. He wished he could provide her with a more exciting way to pass the time but his life was spent in the marketplace and he had no idea where to look for diversions.

***

Monday morning was a disappointment. Once more Marion made her pitch and there was little positive reaction. "People are all given out," the man in the blue suit who always sat in the front shouted. She wanted to point to the millions of dollars spent on DVDs and alcohol and cigarettes but she knew the answer. *We need our comforts and those people are far away.*

That night she tried to talk to Bernard about it but he was watching the business news and seemed to be depressed. "Truth has been devalued," he murmured.

"Come and talk to me," she suggested. Was she not, after all, in the caring business? What use to care for the starving masses if not for the unhappy soul at home?

She patted the cushion beside her as if asking a dog to come and join her there. He knelt on the floor and put his head in her lap.

***

Bernard had the feeling when he went into the building next day that someone was waiting behind the door with a hatchet. *Here comes a chopper to chop off your head.* A silly kids' game played now by grown-ups and called down-sizing. In his own office he sat down and pulled out from his store of dreams the small manageable farm on one of the Gulf Islands. He saw himself milking goats and churning the result for hours till it coagulated. Marion would pack the cheese into cute decorated jars and sell it at the local market. The sun always shone in that dream and all the goats were amiable.

★★★

"He's remote," Marion said to the counsellor.

"Will you sleep with me?" the counsellor asked.

"Certainly not," Marion replied very sharply, wondering to whom she could report this unprofessional professional.

"I only asked if you'd like some tea," the man replied. "Is it a problem? Did you once have a traumatic experience related to that beverage? Tell me about it."

Uncertain whether to scream or simply to pour out her troubles, she chose the latter and then decided on both.

★★★

"I think," Bernard said to the boss, "that you are making a mistake."

The boss was wearing a black jacket and grey slacks and a pink striped shirt. His tie was spotted. He frowned and twisted his mouth to one side and then the other, revealing a place under his chin that the razor had missed. Grey stubble. Unsightly.

"I don't believe that," he replied. "All my decisions are based on careful thought. And when I say you are fired."

He stopped. Three moments passed. Then a fourth. And a fifth.

Bernard waited and then stared. The man's mouth was open but no sound was coming out of it. His eyes were asking for help. Bernard reached for the phone and told the receptionist to call an ambulance quickly.

"What have you done to him?" she asked.

He touched the man. Nothing in his body seemed to be moving except his pulse. The chest was rising and falling.

Others entered the room and looked at Bernard as though he were responsible.

"In mid-sentence," he said. "Just like that. I'd only told him he was making a mistake."

"Ah!" The monosyllable seemed to come from a chorus.

★★★

Advice! Marion had never been good at accepting advice. It was another thing she knew about herself besides the way she sometimes turned from a serious discussion by making a flippant remark. And the counsellor had told her two things: that she should have her ears checked, and that she should learn to rely on others. He hadn't given her the names and phone numbers of any reliable 'others'.

Back in her office, tallying up the week's lack of success, she broke into tears, wiped her face quickly, sniffed and sighed, and put a call through to Bernard's office only to be told to get off the line. There was an emergency. Someone was ill.

She rushed out to her car and drove too quickly to the Keever Building. The ambulance was pulling away, sirens screaming. She made a U-turn and followed it through red lights till it pulled up at the hospital. Parked outside Emergency, she waited till the paramedics unloaded the stretcher and then bent down to look at her beloved's face.

"That's not my husband," she said.

The men answered gently, "Just wait in reception till you're called, ma'am."

★★★

Bernard called Marion's office and found that she had run out in a panic. What was it all about? Was one of the kids ill? He phoned for a cab. There was no one at home. No note. Nothing.

★★★

He waited for an hour and then went to the hospital to check up on the boss. He walked down corridors that smelled of antiseptic and death. And there was Marion sitting by the man's bed in the holding area. Was she his lover? Had they unbelievably – the man was a blustering toad – been having an affair? How could she have known he was here unless there was some bond between them? The stroke had only happened a couple of hours ago. He was backing out of the place when she called his name.

"Bernard!"

"Marion!"

"I thought it was you," she said.

He looked at the man's frozen features and then considered what he knew his own face to be. "I don't look like that."

He sifted quickly through a list of responses to the obvious situation: Immediate forgiveness. Frosty rejection. Hurt. He could feel all the years of love and strain, all the Christmas mornings spent trying to thaw a frozen turkey, crises with the kids, floods in the basement, breaking into pieces like a shattered vase. He wanted to sit on the hospital floor and cry but he said calmly, "Why?"

"It happens," she replied. "Stress. Heredity. Who knows?"

"You could have told me."

The boss's wife came in and rushed to the silent man on the bed, kissed his cheeks, held his hand.

"I stayed till you came," Marion told her and then got up to go. "I followed the ambulance because." She looked at Bernard and tears came to her eyes.

On the drive home, she reached for his hand at the light. And he knew that what he felt was remorse for his lack of faith.

He could wait till they were sitting down after dinner with a cup of coffee to tell her his news.

The fire engine was outside the house when they drove up. Alastair and Jeannie had set the kitchen alight trying to make fries. Not much damage had been done but the stove was wrecked, the wall behind it was black and the bitter smell of burnt fat drove them upstairs. Marion was pleased that the kids had at least tried to make themselves a meal. They were old enough now to do more round the house. She would rely on them. And on Bernard. If she took a break from work, she could spend time at the gym, the art gallery, the movies.

Alastair promised to clean up the mess tomorrow.

★★★

In bed that night she said, "It's been a pretty awful day. But we survived."

Bernard fished around for the right words. *I am about to be fired. I'll have no job. I'll be a drag on the market. I'm going to make a new start.*

Finally he said, "Goats. Do you like goats?"

★★★

When he went downstairs next morning, she was scrubbing the kitchen counter. She looked as though she'd been up all night. He gave her a hug and she leaned on him.

"Goats smell," she said.

★★★

He went to work early with those two words in his mind. If he was cheerful, nonchalant, they would think he had another job lined up and didn't care whether he got the sack or not. The deputy boss summoned him before he'd even begun to pack his photographs and special pens.

He strode into the man's office briskly as if he'd been interrupted while making an important transaction. "Yes?" he said sharply.

"What were you thinking?" the deputy asked.

"Goats smell," Bernard said and turned and walked away.

The words echoed round the fifth floor. The deputy boss and two board members came to Bernard's office that afternoon and stood in the doorway.

"You were absolutely right, Bernie," the senior member announced, "when you said, 'Don't sell.'"

★★★

Marion was in a great mood. "We'll celebrate," she said. "Take the kids out. We can't eat at home anyway." Rain had been falling for seven days in a remote part of Bangladesh. A thousand people were homeless. An unknown number were feared drowned. There were pictures on TV every hour. Money was pouring in so fast that she'd had to stay late at the office.

"Yes," Bernard said. "That's fine." In his mind, he was responding to a possible question from a business reporter. *To what do you attribute your sudden rise in the company? To truth,* he will reply.

Starry Night

ANTONIA WAS DISSATISFIED. In all her thirty-one years she had done nothing amazing. Climbers in Nepal edged their way up the side of Mount Everest because it was there. Below the sea, divers in wetsuits, strapped to oxygen tanks, went to great depths to prove that they could. In caves, crawling on their bellies, men and women sought new and narrower openings in the earth. There was much striving going on high and low all over the world. Danger was courted. Admirers spent their money not on flowers and chocolates but on boots and tents and lights and ropes and hats and dried stew. They offered all those things and more, sometimes even their lives, to the object of their love.

★★★

"I haven't striven," she said as she turned the music down.

Why did she and her friends need such loud background sound to live by? When they were fifty they would surely move to a quieter, slower beat and at seventy they might have slowed to a crawl. It was time perhaps for her to take to the air in a balloon or learn to fly a fragile plane: anything to go further and higher and stay wherever it was for longer.

"It's not for everybody," Parvati replied.

"Life is passing me by."

"You are passing life by."

They were sitting side by side on the couch in Antonia's apartment looking out at the sky and drinking beer. This really wasn't a discussion to have with Parvati because Parvati was practical and didn't have time for dreams. Although that wasn't fair. Parvati thought that if you worked hard and cared for family and friends, fantastic things could happen. It was simply important not to expect them.

They'd finished clearing up after last night's party. Seventeen people. Beer and wine. Lamb korma, couscous, salad. A birthday cake with too many candles. Four dishwasher loads and a mess of icing to clean off the rug.

"Alexander was dead by the time he was my age."

"So now you want to be a soldier."

"Maybe an explorer. Not much is undiscovered."

"To paraphrase an idiot, you don't know what you don't know."

"Another beer?"

Parvati shook her head. She had work to do and was going home. She touched Antonia on the shoulder and said, "Be a star-gazer."

★★★

It had been a great party. All of the guests were between the ages of 28 and 35. All were technically single though twelve of them lived with partners so might as well be married. All were employed in one way and another. They had space, they earned enough to support themselves and to enjoy their leisure time in modest ways. They owned no yachts or private planes but mainly spent their vacations camping or at family cottages. All of them were more or less good-looking. Parvati with her long dark hair and deep brown eyes was even lovely. Antonia herself, she knew, was 'handsome': good features, blonde, tall, not bad.

Sitting alone in the aftermath, she heard yesterday's voices as if all the laughter and music still lurked in the corners and a ghostly party continued. But there was doubt in the echoes. Little stings of loneliness, futility, even of fear. It wasn't only the alcohol leaving its sloth and slight depression. She truly wanted to ask – and the question had been in the air last night too – what am I doing here? In other words, is this it?

She threw the rest of the beer down the sink and decided to make a cup of strong coffee. While the kettle boiled, she stared out of the window at the world below. The city was hot. It was *foetid*. That was the word. Pollutants trapped in these long cement corridors were assaulting the lungs of the innocent and the guilty alike: those who rode bicycles and those who drove big cars. As for pedestrians . . .

Who were all those people, and what made them walk up and down Yonge Street in such a hurry like a crowd of wind-up toys? To what purpose? What did they want? The ones going south like lemmings were perhaps intent on throwing themselves into Lake Ontario. She had never seen a lemming and wondered whether anyone had tried to stop them in their march to self-destruction and what, if they'd been turned back, the little animals would have done with the rest of their lives.

★★★

Tomorrow she'd be back in the office and her only struggle there was to make it to upper management by the time she was forty. The work was routine with only an occasional week or two of excitement when there was a large estate to settle. In other words, life was fun when someone croaked. She sat back feeling more depressed than ever. She drank the coffee quickly, not wanting to stay in a room that still smelled of tobacco and beer.

Putting on her sandals, she went outside to join those heading north towards forest and lake and isolation. If they kept walking up Yonge Street day after day, they would get to Barrie and North Bay and then the wilderness. Deciduous trees would give way to tall evergreens and rocks, then to smaller, sparser firs and at last they would be beyond the line of trees. But most were probably only going to the subway or to stores or to find their parked cars. A few of them perhaps had plans for the longer trek, their aim to get as far as they could before the poisonous air killed them and they lay dead in heaps on the hot concrete.

It was getting dark but there was no promise of a cool night ahead.

She kept walking till her shirt was sticking to her breasts and her armpits. Her sandals seemed to have a purpose as if they were on their way to see the wizard who could answer the great question. The thud of last night's music gave her a beat to march by. She was faster than most of the others going her way and very few overtook her. As she turned on to Yorkville, she looked up to see whether the first star had yet appeared.

Light flashed in her face and someone said, "Get out of here." She tripped over a cable, took a few steps to right herself, and fell into the arms of the handsomest man she had ever, she thought, so far seen. A late birthday gift?

"Hello," she said.

"Get her out of here."

"We're shooting," the handsome fellow said, tightening his grip.

She was about to apologise when another voice beyond the light shouted, "If you're Mandy, you're late. Get over here."

"I'm not."

"You are late."

She left the handsome man and moved towards the voice. She was pushed into a trailer and handed a tray of make-up and told to 'fix him' because he was sweating. The star came in and sat in front of the mirror. She knew who he was. Famous but said to be charming. While she dabbed at his nose, she heard herself asking the usual dumb questions.

"It's representation," he said. "A truly unreal life. Now you, you go about in the real world all day. Things happen around you. I go about pretending."

"Have you ever climbed a mountain?"

"Did you see *Heights*? I had a double in the fall scene. The guy slipped into the crevasse. Broke both legs. I felt guilty for days."

He was wearing a hairpiece and she could see that if she wiped all the colour off his face he would be quite plain.

A man stuck his head round the trailer door and said, "For Chrissake you've made him look like a pastry."

Antonia dabbed at the face again and they went out into the light. A man came by carrying a head that was a bloody replica of the star's.

She'd stumbled into make-believe and it wasn't what she was looking for at all. A woman stopped her and said, "You're not Mandy, you're that journalist. Get off the set before I have you thrown off."

"I'm not," she protested for the second time.

But it wasn't a place where truth counted.

★★★

She stepped back to join the crowd of watchers on the other sidewalk.

A man beside her said, "It's his first horror movie."

"Oh," she answered.

"Exciting. Watching it being put together. Slow. They go over every scene a dozen times. Trying to get it exactly right. There he comes now. Look. Watch what he does when he looks at his own corpse."

It was a horrible moment.

She gasped. The stranger held her arm and began to tell her about the star's failing fourth marriage, the pregnant maid, and three different custody battles. Then he was silent. She looked round and he was gone.

***

She was close to her mother's apartment block and it wasn't too late to go and tell her about this little adventure. They would laugh over it together. When she got to the building, she pressed the number on the entry pad beside the door. There was no response. It was after ten. Sunday night. Where was her mother? Playing bridge with her friend in the apartment down the hall most likely. Antonia reached into her bag for her cell phone. Not there. No wallet either. She dug down into all the pockets of the purse. Nothing. The chatty stranger was a thief!

She sat on the wall of the well-kept little garden in front of the building and considered all that had to be done. Cancel the credit card. Get a new driving licence. The bank card! That man could be emptying her account even now. Except that he didn't know the code. But he had all her other information and by morning he could be Antonia Warne. She felt around for her keys and they too were gone. Tears were rising but she sniffed and held them back. A quarter would get her to Parvati and Parvati would pick her up and help her.

A woman walked by with her dog.

"Please," Antonia begged, "Could you let me have a quarter for the phone."

The woman walked quickly on tugging at the dog's lead.

I'm destitute. I'm a beggar. I'm despised.

Her feet were tired but there was nothing for it but to plod back to her apartment and ask the janitor to let her in. Proof of identity? None. *But you know me. I live here.*

Still sitting on the wall, she considered continuing to go north, hitching a ride to the place where lakes were still pristine and where true darkness revealed ten thousand more stars than you could ever see in the city.

A man walked up to the door of the building.

"My mother lives in here," she said to him. "She's in her friend's apartment and."

He opened the door quickly and sidled in, shutting her out.

She began to wonder about her appearance. Did she really look like a street person? She hadn't changed out of the old shirt she'd been wearing to clean the apartment, a shirt belonging to her last 'relationship'. Jeff. Her shorts were ripped-off jeans, not even neatly cut. Yes, she looked like a vagrant.

OK. List of options. Keep hoping some kind stranger would give her a quarter. Start walking back home. Stop a cop and tell him of the theft. (In these clothes would he even believe she owned such a thing as a credit card?) Wait for a miracle to happen.

She got up to join the night crowd making its way towards the lake.

★★★

Notes of loud music shrieked out from passing cars. A woman with a megaphone was exhorting everyone to be saved. Antonia stopped to see where the voice was coming from. A man shoved her and she fell against the wall. It was too much. She grabbed at him.

"Why don't you look where you're going?"

"I'm sorry," he said.

"Oh," she replied, startled because she'd expected aggression and had been ready for a fight and was all set to punch him if need be. "Then perhaps you could let me have a quarter."

He gave her a dollar coin and moved on.

"No," she called after him. "I want a quarter."

He walked away more quickly, obviously considering her deranged.

She looked at the dollar and felt its shape and raised design. It was treasure.

The wall by the apparatus was covered in graffiti. She keyed in the number and put in the coin. Her friend's voice suggested that she leave a message.

"I know you're there. Pick up the phone."

She pressed the coin return button. There was nothing in the little box. She had spent her treasure for nothing.

Passing Yorkville, she returned to the movie set. A small group was still watching the scene.

"I was robbed here," she yelled out. "Watch out for a man who stands too close."

A Mountie came towards her. She wasn't sure whether to cut and run or to tell him her sad tale and hope to be believed. *Young woman shot dead in street running from police. Drugs thought to be a factor.*

"I'm glad to see you," she said to him.

★★★

It took more than an hour at the police station to tell her story and convince them that she was indeed herself. The Mountie, detailed to keep an eye on the star, had called another cop to come to her aid. Suspicion was the natural mindset of the keepers of law and order. They wanted to know why she had moved away from the scene of the crime. If she really had been robbed, why had she let so much time go by before asking for help?

"I didn't know I'd been robbed till I got to my mother's place!" she repeated over and over. Two drunks were brought in, one bleeding from a cut on his face. A handcuffed woman being led away called out to her for help. The place smelled of vomit and despair. She wanted to scream but screaming might land her in a cell too.

★★★

"I felt," she told her mother, "unbelieved and therefore unbelievable. I was unreal for a while."

Her mother, driving her back home, let the question of why her daughter was out on the street in those clothes hang in the air.

"I hope I'm not going to have to bail you out often, sweetheart."

"You didn't 'bail' me out."

This was going to be a family story now. *The night I had to get Antonia out of jail.* Jokes and sly remarks would come at her like hailstones. Thanksgiving would be hell.

★★★

At the office next morning, Parvati whispered, "You look terrible. What were you doing last night?"

"I took your advice. I star-gazed."

At that moment, climbers were ambling down mountains, divers paddling to the surface, and cavers slithering up to the light. For all their efforts, none of them had likely found the answer to the big question. And to her, only one thing had been made clear: from now on she must always carry a pocket full of change.

The Worrier

"Stop that row," Angharad calls from the kitchen. "You're curdling the soup."

Bendrix does not stop. He has told her before that when he promises his clients an hour, that's what they get. It's a matter of trust, of not short-changing the customer. He keeps on painting the bathroom wall a pale shade of pink and wails more loudly. He is multi-tasking. When he has given the Bowdlers their full time on the possibility of the NDP winning the next election, he will wash the roller and then allow half an hour for his own thoughts. He does for a moment manage to squeeze in a wish that Angharad wouldn't make chowder. He can smell the fishy sliminess of it and does not look forward to dinner.

Angharad is aware that by giving up his practice, the office on 17th Avenue, firing his receptionist, and becoming a professional worrier, Bendrix is earning more money. He is paying the mortgage down. They will soon own the house. But she wishes he had more time to think about her and her problems. She writes notes to remind him to have sex; these are her best child-bearing years.

Soon after he took up his new line of work, Bendrix realised that because so many men and women are concerned about the same things, he could worry on several people's behalf at once. He was surprised at first that in this unstructured set-up, most of his clients would pay on time and even in advance.

He supposes it's because they're afraid: if he stops working on their behalf, their worries might return home to them like bricks thrown at their heads. Thump. Thump. Thump.

He charges extra for wailing and gnashing of teeth. Fortunately there is not much call for the latter as his mouth is still tender from the last root canal procedure.

After ten years as a psychiatrist, it dawned on him one day that he could help people without having to see them. No more pushing a box of Kleenex across the table to a weepy man or hearing another boring tale of infidelity, no more choking back the urge to shout, *Get a life, why don't you,* at the body on the couch. Now, for an hourly rate, he will worry by proxy about the starving in Africa, the trouble in Afghanistan, the state of the health system. His clients email their concerns to him. He can spend an hour fretting about the war in Iraq on behalf of several people at once and collect multiple fees. Here at home he can do his chores while he works. It's a beautiful arrangement.

He helps Angharad tidy the kitchen after dinner and settles down to three hours solid agonising over nuclear waste, the trouble in the Sudan and the state of the stock market. No wailing required. Just truly dedicated concern.

The phone rings. He lets Angharad answer it and can see when she comes into the room that it's trouble. He marks the time in his notebook so that he can pick up where he left off, and waits.

She hands him the phone as if it's a dirty thing and says, "Laurel."

He almost doesn't take it from her but then Laurel would only call again. His ex-wife is a persistent woman.

"I wish," Angharad says, "that . . . "

He waves her away.

Laurel, now the CEO of her own health food company, has likely not called to talk to him about the suffering of the world.

She is possessive, can't bear to let go of anything she has once owned. The words, *it's over, honey,* have not sunk into her consciousness. He agrees to meet for breakfast next morning just so that she will leave him alone to get on with his work.

***

Laurel looks – he finds a word – 'vibrant'. She is wearing a blue jacket and shirt and there is an electricity about her that is repellent and exciting at the same time. He wishes he hadn't come and chews into his bagel so that he doesn't have to talk.

Bendrix has taken a weight off her friend's mind, she says, and he must do the same for her. She fears that her young lover, Joel, will leave her. She's not sleeping and her concentration is slipping. She hasn't been to the gym in days. If she could only set this problem aside, her life would return to normal. Bendrix tells her he doesn't do small, and asks the obvious question: Why doesn't she tackle Joel and find out one way or another?

Before she leaves, Laurel gives him samples of her rejuvenating products: all that worrying has aged him. She pats his hand and thanks him for his time. Then she gets out a professional-looking camera and takes a picture of him.

Bendrix finds himself sitting alone in the cafe thinking about Laurel and Joel. He is in fact pondering all that is on her mind: profit and loss. The success or failure of the new pomegranate drink. The colour of her new outfit. The advantages of Botox injections.

He understands there and then that a terrible thing has happened to him. Every single item she mentioned has seeped into his brain. He has become a worry magnet. People only have to hint at their problems and, like a computer, his mind stores them. He takes inventory. It's too much. He feels his synapses snapping at one another. His hard drive is overloaded.

The waitress comes to him with a glass of water and says, "What was she saying to you? You look terrible."

★★★

At home, he goes into the worry room, a converted closet, and looks at his schedule for the coming week. Nine or ten hours of straight worry every day. The doorbell rings. Elsa from the other half of the duplex is standing on the step. She looks distraught. Because he's now at home in the daytime, she comes round whenever she needs help reaching for something off a high shelf or to change a light bulb. Sometimes she complains about the noise.

"I won't be wailing today," he tells her.

"It's not that," she says. "I've got used to it. I know you do it to help people. I'm worried about my pension, Bendrix. And my son is getting a divorce . . . "

"No!" he shouts and closes the door in her face. One more worry added to the load in his head and he would crash.

★★★

That afternoon, Angharad comes to him, her lovely face wearing a stark, mean expression.

"After my Dad's visit, I'm leaving."

"I can't think about that right now," he replies. "I'm worrying."

"Not only are you totally paying no attention to me. You've been unkind to Elsa."

"I'll explain later. But right now . . . "

"Go and meet my Dad at the airport," she says. "Be nice to him. And next week I'm out of here."

★★★

While driving, Bendrix found he could manage twenty minutes for Genna Blackstein's worry about fish stocks in the seas around Newfoundland. At the same time, he allows into a fragment of unoccupied space a visual impression of the foothills, the mountains beyond, and clouds that suggest snow is on the way.

★★★

Mr. Jones comes through the security door pulling a large red case on wheels. If Bendrix had had the capacity, he would have worried about the projected length of the old preacher's visit. Mr. Jones introduces the woman beside him as his fellow passenger and says to her, "This is the man who lives in sin with my daughter."

On the drive home, Bendrix asks about the journey and shuts out Mr. Jones's list of complaints about the food on the plane, the service, and the delay at Manchester. Since the old man never stops talking and requires no response, it's easy to ignore him.

★★★

Later, Bendrix keeps on with his assignments while Mr. Jones tells Angharad all the news from the unpronounceable little town in Wales they call home. He has learnt how to keep a slight smile on his face while worrying. It fools people into thinking that he is paying attention. Angharad knows he is not. He does hear Mr. Jones say, while he's spooning up his raspberry mousse, that his church has given him a month's leave, and registers Angharad's look of despair.

Mr. Jones has more than once threatened to marry them whether they like it or not. Bendrix imagines a ceremony performed in the dark while he and Angharad are asleep, or awake just enough to say, *I do,* with the old man waving his hands over them and singing Welsh hymns.

The next afternoon, Angharad is called to the hospital to fill in for a sick colleague. After dinner, Bendrix sits back in the rocker and closes his eyes. While Mr. Jones talks on in the background he can get on with his work: the Patriot Act in the U.S. and the Prime Minister's approach to the Health Service.

He is well into it when he hears the old man in his lilting accent shouting directly into his ear, "Getting deaf are you? Tell me what's on your mind, boy. Aside from the fact that you are living in sin with my daughter. A fact which must weigh heavy on your conscience. And which I would like to remedy while I am here. I can see that my daughter is not happy. And there is good reason for that. Sin is a worm which can gnaw at the soul and destroy peace and contentment. Utterly. Not only in the here but also in the hereafter. Staying in this house is a penance for me but I will stay until I have . . . "

"Shut up," Bendrix cries. And then apologises.

"So," the old man says again, "tell me what's on your mind, boy."

★★★

When Angharad returns at midnight she's surprised to see Bendrix making cocoa for her father. He is stirring hot milk into the mug and smiling.

"Hello, darling," he says, and kisses her lovingly.

In the living room, her father is kneeling on the floor in prayer. His shoulders are hunched over as if they bear the weight of the world and he is trying to pass the burden on to God. After a while he stands up and accepts the cocoa without thanks.

"In Wales, we sing," he says. "We sing about our sorrows. But sometimes there are so many, that we lose our voice."

He asks for biscuits. He always eats two digestives before bed.

"What it is, you see," Mr. Jones goes on, "is that you have no right to take on somebody else's burden unless you can in fact do something about it. There is deception otherwise. There is fraud. No good is being done." He sighs and is silent. And remains silent. Says no more.

★★★

Next morning, in comes Laurel with her camera. She kisses Bendrix.

"My wife," Bendrix says to Mr. Jones.

"You look wonderful," Laurel says to him. "It's the pomegranate juice."

The camera flashes in his face. "Before and After," she says.

"It's only been two days," he tells her.

"Get out," Angharad says and punches Laurel's shoulder, "and take your fucking juice with you."

Bendrix laughs.

Mr. Jones looks as though he has been struck on either cheek with a wet fish.

Laurel is picking her camera up from the floor. She looks at Bendrix for sympathy, defence, anything. He waves goodbye and means it.

"This is how we live," he says to Mr. Jones after the door has banged shut.

And to Angharad he says, "Let's go away for a few days, my love, and think about the future which you can translate as making love day and night."

Mr. Jones groans.

Bendrix hugs him and says, "You have done me a great service. If I could write music and, who knows, perhaps I can, I would write a song for you."

★★★

Driving from Calgary to Banff, he says to Angharad, "I told your Dad to visit Elsa next door while we're gone. She needs help."

"I just hope he'll remember to feed the cat."

"He has a lot on his mind, sweetheart."

That evening, a glass of wine in his hand, he puts his feet up on the couch in their suite and thinks. He has been worrying since he was five years old, perhaps four. And the worries escalated as he worked his way from kindergarten through the torturous maze of the education system. Homework, girls, exams, the football team, acne, his parents' divorce. To cap it all, he chose a profession that allowed others to pass their problems on to him. He has had, till now, no peace. But here, the mountains only a dark shape in the distance, Angharad changing into something lacy in the bathroom, he has nothing at all on his mind but sex. It is a lovely moment. One that the five-year-old wearing his little backpack and trotting into the maw of a classroom for the first time could not have imagined.

He takes off all his clothes, closes his eyes, and waits. She is taking a long time. No doubt she is smearing herself with a tantalising oil.

He hears footsteps. Listens closely. Dread! It is not only the light steps of his beloved that he can hear. Accompanying her, he can tell, are the leaden footfalls of her aggravating Welsh conscience. It appears beside her at the most inconvenient times.

"We've left my dad on his own," she is saying, "in a strange place."

Bendrix draws on all his psychiatric training. He puts his arms round her and lifts her off the ground and says, "I want you."

***

The house has a different look to it when they return. The paint on the woodwork is the same colour. The shrubs either side of the steps haven't moved. And yet all is not right. Angharad, holding his hand, hasn't noticed anything. She is still slightly glazed from wine and sex. He opens the door gingerly, inch by inch.

The sound of organ music fills the hall. Words in the language he knows to be Welsh accompany it. There are lace curtains hanging in the windows. No one can see in or out. The couch has been moved to the centre of the living room. A smell of roast beef drifts towards them.

"Hello!" he shouts.

"What's going on?" Angharad says.

Bendrix feels as if a flock of birds is flying round his head, trying to get in, pecking, scratching. He tries to brush them away.

Mr. Jones is lying on the couch listening to music coming from the CD player. He turns towards them and motions them to be silent. In the kitchen, Elsa in a red sweater and black skirt is cooking. There is a glass of wine beside her on the counter.

"Your dad's quite a guy," she says to Angharad.

"What's going on?" Angharad repeats.

Bendrix, fearing the worst, takes their bags into the bedroom. Has the old man sawed their bed down the middle or moved in two singles? No! The room looks just the same except for a piece of paper tacked on the wall at his side of the bed. It is an account for several hours of 'concern on behalf of others'. He took another look at the bed. The sheets were rumpled and both pillows were dented.

"You've got it all wrong, boy," the old man says when he returns to the living room. "What it is, you see, is the appearance of things. You might think, returning too soon as you have, that your neighbour and I have taken over your house. This is only partly true. Just as people seeing you and my daughter living here together, might think you are married.

"As for the work you took upon yourself, I have only one thing to say: you are not God. I advise you to go for a humbler profession. There is always a need for bus drivers. As for the other matter, I would only ask you to consider the children."

★★★

Two weeks later at the airport, Angharad cries a little when she says goodbye to her dad. She waves, showing off the gold band on her finger. He walks through the security gate like a man who has been and seen and learnt something. Bendrix, watching the back of his father-in-law, smiles.

He and Angharad will take down the lacy drapes from the windows. He will set up his computer in the guest bedroom and continue to work at home: there is a contract for two self-help books on his desk. 'Productive Worrying' is the working title of the first one. The second will be called, 'I am not God and neither, by the way, are you.'

Kindness

"WHAT WAS YOUR FAVOURITE TOY when you were a child?"

Martina looked at the man. He was height-deprived, fifty-ish; a small know-it-all conscious of his ten years of higher education. He had beaver teeth. It was surprising that his lips could meet. Perhaps he chewed wood for a hobby. For all the certificates on his wall testifying that Dr. Jean-Claude Vauguard was an expert in medicine and psychiatry, he would never understand why she wasn't going to fall for a question like that. She picked up her purse and made for the door. Behind her he was likely marking down her response as denial. She smiled at the receptionist, took her coat from the stand and, as she ran down the steps, laughed. She had just wasted a hundred dollars on a non-therapy session. With that money she could replace her favourite toy, even at today's prices.

★★★

It was raining but not hard. She turned up her face to catch the drops and remarked to the sky, "I am sane."

★★★

In the store, she looked at the talking dolls and the trucks and the green monsters, fought off the helpful sales staff who wanted to know the age of the child she was shopping for, and found a box marked, 'Theatre'. It had a brightly coloured picture of a proscenium arch on the front and contained, so it promised, three plays for young people.

"I'll take this," she said.

"Your daughter's interested in theatre?"

"How do you know it isn't my son?"

"After thirty years in the business, we've come to know what girls like and what appeals to the boys."

Still with the stereotypes. Dolls for girls. Soldiers for boys. Did nothing change? Martina refrained from saying, I am a childless, single woman suffering from sorrow and this is for me. She put her card down on the counter, mentally adding up the total spent so far this month. Too much. Beyond the limit. Then she recalled her inheritance and bought an expensive remote-controlled tank.

"That's for my niece," she told the sales clerk as she set it down on the counter.

★★★

She opened her apartment door and tried not to inhale. The air was a miasma of used breath, smells from different re-heated meals, and a hint of sweetness from the hyacinth in its pot on the table. Keeping her coat on, she opened the window wide. And then, deciding she could deal with trouble if it arrived in the shape of nosy neighbours, felonious intruders, the landlord, she propped the door ajar. A through draft. A draft through the place. Maybe the sea, two kilometres away, would send a pleasing breeze and saltily cleanse the air and her mind. Not till later would she open the package from the toy store. That would be a reward for work completed. She sat down at the computer and brought up John Witlock's file. And remembered that she'd had no lunch.

Nonetheless, to work! 'The yellow dog,' she typed, 'walked slowly down the road.'

There was a chocolate bar in the top drawer of the desk. She broke a piece off and ate it. 'The dog is the subject of that sentence,' she went on, 'qualified by the adjective *yellow*. The verb *walked* tells us what the dog is doing.'

★★★

No wonder she was depressed. These kids should read. Read books. Read newspapers. Read magazines. But parents were willing to pay for virtual lessons so that their offspring could advance through life without going to the library, without knowing poetry, without ever, beyond school, reading one single novel for pleasure. John Witlock was sixteen and had travelled thus far through the system without being able to parse a simple sentence. Why did his parents not enroll him in a handicraft class? Let him learn to do something useful. Teach him to knit. '*Walked*, John, is the past tense of the verb *to walk*.'

Walking away is cowardly but sometimes it is the only option.

This was her last attempt to educate the young. Soon she'd be back at the office, working with grown-ups who talked about gerunds and the subjunctive. The second time he'd found her staring blankly at a manuscript, Harry said, "Take some time off. Don't come back till you've had a good cry."

John Witlock could be the one to bring on her tears.

★★★

"Hello. You in there?" Too late she remembered the open door.

"I'm working," she called back.

"It's Tuesday."

Althea came in and closed the door behind her.

"It's freezing in here."

Martina got up and closed the window.

"So it's Tuesday?"

"I knew you'd forget."

While Althea drove along Beach Drive, Martina looked at the sea and wished she was on a ship to Africa instead of on her way to meet a man who professed to cure all by Yogic exercise and meditation. Perhaps he would induce her to relax deeply so that her tears would fall and make a pool on the floor. Or will Yoga, she wondered, make me easier to get along with? Will it bring me friends galore? Will it reduce my ambitions to nothing more than the desire to be able to thread a piece of dental floss up one nostril and down the other?

She no longer felt hungry.

★★★

Grief. That was what had brought her to be sitting in a car beside a woman she didn't particularly like. Sympathy was a hard thing to fight against. The word alone sounded like a cushion. Kindness, gentle phrases, flowers, *I'm sorry about your mother*; all were traps. It was hard to respond by saying, I'm fine thank you, without sounding heartless.

Althea had been the first to come and bring her a casserole. She had followed this with a little visit every other day. A loaf of home-made bread. A bottle of wine. Overwhelming consideration. *Your mother was good to me.* She began to wonder whether Althea had any other friends.

Her dislike was irrational. Althea in her brown jacket and neatly tied scarf had a pleasing profile, round cheeks, small nose, and was a decent woman. She taught grades three and four at the local school. But it was now three weeks since the funeral and she was still playing the part of a social worker. Her goodness was repellent. There were seven more school-free weeks to go, time in which she could devote herself to her prey. Martina recalled a Leonard Cohen song, *Let me go while you can.* Or was it, *Before it's too late?* Or, *Before I kill you?*

Her real friends called and offered to go with her to movies, lunch, the book sale, and weren't offended when she drew back and said next week perhaps. They didn't persist but would be there when she needed them.

***

The yoga teacher was a man of about thirty. He hugged them both, kissed Althea, and showed them where to put their raincoats. Martina was ready to leave but she'd run away once today and decided to go through with the lesson. She paid Sanjeet for six sessions but knew she was throwing the money away. On the way home, she would say that she was all right now, she could grieve competently alone, and that Althea should get on with her own life. Surely there were other people who needed her help. Perhaps she could give the woman a gift, something that would absolutely and unequivocally say, 'Leave me alone': a potted cactus or a large bottle of cheap scent.

***

She was lying on the floor on a mat that had been no doubt used by countless others. Mites from their skin were probably crawling onto hers, colonising her back and neck. Her head was supposed to be empty and her limbs reduced to rubber. Sanjeet was white, his name adopted from another culture, and he was intoning a mantra: You are relaxed. You are perfectly relaxed. His eyes were closed. Althea beside her was perfecting the corpse pose. Somewhere in India, temple bells were ringing and women in bright saris were swaying to the music of sitars. After a few minutes in which her muscles seemed to get tighter and tighter, Martina very quietly got to her knees and then to her feet. She picked up her shoes and took her coat and purse from the hook and slunk out.

The note she left on Althea's windshield simply said, "I'll call you next week." There was no need of explanation.

***

At five o'clock she was at the other building, in number 5a, her mother's condo. It was time to move on; a shame to leave it empty when space at this price was so much in demand. So said the helpful relatives and especially her brother who wanted his half of the money. And now here was the agent turning up her nose at the old-fashioned furniture, the dark paint, the small windows. Martina was about to say, I'll leave you to look round, you've got a key. And then she realised that if she did, she would be walking away for the third time in one single day. One period of eight hours. *Avoidance* would become her middle name. She would be called *unreliable.* She took off her coat and remembered her father's motto: *Always ask for more than you think you'll get.*

The agent was a woman about her own age, obviously selling at the low end of the property market. She needed help. She was smartly dressed and probably drove a car she could barely afford in order to appear successful. Her card said she was Hilary Greene and there was no reason to doubt it.

"Ms. Greene," Martina said, "I need the capital from this. There is no mortgage. Tell me if there's anything I can do to help make it easier to sell other than offer it at a ridiculous price."

"You will clear the furniture out?"

"Of course."

"And clean it."

"There's a sea view for Christ's sake. What more do you want!"

***

After Hilary Greene had gone, Martina wished she had skipped out. Daunting – the idea of emptying the place, sweeping it, rubbing away her mother's fingerprints. She sat down in the heavy brown plush rocking chair, rested her hands on its wooden arms and faced the window. Tears were dripping down the glass outside. *You're so good to me, Marti.* But those were not her mother's words. The reality had been different. *I have to rely on my neighbours. You're never here.* Twice a week she'd listened to that refrain and it stuck in her mind like an advertising jingle. *You're never here.* And so she'd hurried through her visits every Wednesday and Saturday always looking for errands to do, filling in the time. She was the delinquent daughter who visited but was not present.

Althea, the good child, unrelated, divorced, tenant of the apartment below, found her still sitting there.

"I'll help you clear it out. I do understand why you had to leave, honey."

She put her arm round Martina's shoulders and gave them a squeeze.

It was too much.

"You were kind to my mother," Martina said. "I'd like to give you something of hers."

"It was enough to know that she was my friend. And now you're my friend. What better legacy could there be?"

"You are too good, Althea," Martina said, "Really, really too good. I want you to have her rocking chair. I'll help you move it to the elevator."

"What do you mean? Oh no. I can't take it. No!"

Martina, using the chair, pushed Althea to the door and out into the hall. Althea had no choice but to hang on to the back of it and, when the elevator door opened, allow herself to be propelled inside. Martina watched the elevator door close on the good woman. She rushed back to the apartment, locked the door, and ran down the stairs.

"I'm not running away," she said to herself. "I'm running towards."

She jogged part of the way through the damp evening and then walked home slowly, enjoying a freedom that was entirely new.

She had been tied to her mother with an umbilical cord that was never severed till now. Her uncles had come to the funeral, two aunts and three cousins. Her brother had cried. She had not. She'd bought plates of meat and cheese from the delicatessen and served wine. It had been a strange party. Silence at first, then murmured words of sympathy and after that family chatter, memories. Uncle Geoff told a few jokes and as he was leaving advised Martina to find a good man; she would have a little money now. She didn't tell him she had a good man but that he was at the other side of the world.

She considered going to a club wearing a T-shirt that said, 'Have money, am available'.

But it wasn't enough money. And buying a man hardly made him a prize. She could probably afford a different man from an escort service once a week, say every Friday, for at least a year. She had seen such men going into number 403, one of them wearing a sweater that said 'NYPD' though New York was two thousand miles away. A pair of handcuffs was clipped to his belt.

Ron in Manila sent random emails. He did call every Sunday to assure her that he loved her and to tell her that he was lonely. She sensed though that the 'dusky maidens' of old adventure stories lurked in the background but said she missed him too.

***

She made herself a sandwich and opened a bottle of beer before she unwrapped the box from the toy store. The little theatre was fancier than the one she'd owned long ago.

The stage folded out and a variety of backdrops could be changed to set the scenes. Tiny figures on sticks portrayed different characters. There was furniture and an assortment of props. The dialogue was written out. One of the plays was, of all things, *Cinderella.*

She set up the scenery. The hearth, the broom. A tiny plastic slipper. The stepmother had wavy dark hair like her mother and would say, No you cannot go to the ball. Who would want to dance with you? The actual words she'd overheard her mother saying once when she was about twenty were, 'Martina isn't what you'd call good-looking, men won't be falling over themselves.' Cinderella's father was a fat version of Dr. Vauguard without the beaver teeth. She cast Althea as both ugly sisters though Althea surely saw herself as a fairy godmother.

"So, Cinderella?" she said to the tiny blonde cut-out. "What's your game plan?"

The fairy godmother, wand and wings and all, flying down to earth on a wire could be a travel agent with a ticket to Manila or Hilary Greene with an offer from a buyer. But the godmother's face became the familiar, concerned face of her mother: for Martina the pumpkin would always be a pumpkin and the mice would never turn into horses. As for the glass slipper, it would forever fit onto someone else's delicate foot.

"I want the best for you," she seemed to be saying.

"I'm all right," Cinderella replied, "really. I am really and truly fine!"

"I only want the best for you," the godmother repeated.

"This is how I am," Martina shouted.

★★★

And then the handsome prince stayed offstage while Cinderella swept the tiny slipper into the ashes and shed tears for her dead mother.

The little theatre gradually became damp and would be no use as a gift for Robert's daughters. Martina dried it with her hair dryer and then crumpled up the tiny figures and threw them in the garbage. One of these days, she would make new characters and write her own script. Meanwhile she emailed a message to Harry: I have wept.

II

Althea pushed the ugly chair into the bedroom out of sight. There was scarcely room between the bed and window. The chest of drawers given to her by Michael Berger after his father's death and the standard lamp that the widower across the hall had left outside her door with a note telling her that he was all right now thank you, took up the rest of the space. She wished people would express their gratitude in smaller ways. The rocker and the lamp between them would bring in fifty dollars and the chest of drawers had an antique look to it and might be worth more but the whole sum wouldn't be enough to dig her out of the current financial mess. Not one of the deceased had thought to mention their dear and kind friend in his or her will: she was a young woman with a good teaching job and a kind heart. Money would have been an insult.

She was in fact a youngish woman without a job and with an excess of time. After she was 'terminated', the union representative said, "We can do nothing. You were fired for cause." And there was rent to be paid. She was one month late already, living on borrowed time in a sublet condo. Life on the street had never appealed to her.

At least Martina was off her hands. She found the woman unresponsive and not at all either friendly or grateful, quite unlike her mother. Mrs. Kraznowski's habit of stopping on the stairs, refusing to take the elevator, had brought the two of them together one morning nearly a year ago. While Mrs. K. got her breath, Althea offered tea and a helping hand. A package of frozen pierogies a few days later was all it had taken to make her into the old lady's dear and indispensable neighbour.

Through the months she'd heard a great deal about the late Mr. K. and their two children. Tad who called himself Robert had taken off to spend six years in Poland and only recently returned with a wife who was beautiful but. The gesture Mrs. K. made with one hand dismissed Hanna as useless and a spendthrift, someone who would drag her son down. Though it seemed to Althea that he hadn't far to go.

The old lady made excuses for 'my daughter Martina, a very busy woman, important job in publishing, very clever, anything to do with language. Unfortunately men don't like clever women. Even nowadays when people are supposed to be equal. But you dear, you must have a man in your life?'

Althea had absorbed the implied insult and only nodded mysteriously and said nothing about Jay or Luke or Matt and particularly Sam.

Mrs. K. hadn't noticed that, long before the end of term, Althea had more time to run errands or that she popped in during the morning on a school day and said, "Do you need anything in town." But by then the old lady was failing. Her mind and her body gradually gave up, quit. The end.

***

She and Sam had enjoyed a good laugh after they heard Martina creep out of the Yoga session. They locked the door and put several mats together and made love. Sanjeet, Althea cried out. Crazy woman, he responded.

"Aren't you going to look for a job?" he asked, giving her half the hundred bucks Martina had paid for a series of classes.

"I get to meet people and besides, I do some good."

"Take a course, be a real social worker."

"This way I get to choose my clients."

"But they don't pay!"

★★★

She sat in the over-padded brown rocker with its dent in the centre cushion, stains on its wooden arms, and faced the future. She missed the old lady and her memories. And the old lady had taken her memories to wherever people went when they died. When they died! Althea's heart shook. She felt it. A shudder like an earthquake tremor went through her body. Somewhere a clock struck. Fifty years passed in five minutes and she was old, alone, depending on a stranger to bring her any comfort, little gifts, news from the world outside. A stranger who perhaps hoped for a legacy and subconsciously willed her to die. She cried for Mrs. K. and for herself and for the unknown. And then she stopped. Tears wouldn't buy food or pay the rent.

Sam/Sanjeet was right. She had to make a life again, go back to work. The reference from the school principal didn't mention the incident and while not enthusiastic did at least call her a reliable teacher. There were schools up island where it was hard to get staff and where she might be welcome. Up Island? Beautiful and remote. She could learn to fish. She could sell herself on her computer skills alone.

★★★

The chair seemed to have closed its arms round her as if it wanted to keep her prisoner. A whole hour had gone by and in that hour she had come to no conclusion. Even if she got a job tomorrow, no one would pay her in advance. What was to be done? Even the image of herself pushing a shopping cart of sad belongings round town didn't produce an idea.

The chair was making her think darkly. It smelled of decay

and the over-scented body of Mrs. K., an old woman so fearful of offensive body odour that she sprayed herself with toilet water several times a day. There was a sadness that Althea couldn't quite pin down but the sense and the scent of it were too much. She jumped up and took hold of the arms of the rocker and said to it, "I don't want you in here. OK! Nothing personal but you're making me morbid."

★★★

In large letters, she printed HELP YOURSELF on a piece of paper and pinned it to the chair-back. She moved the rocker out to the elevator and travelled down with it to the ground floor, out of the main door and onto the sidewalk. Moving it a little to one side of the building to avoid complaints from the manager, she set it against the wall and went back upstairs.

When she went out later to fetch her only decent outfit from the dry cleaners, an elderly man was sitting in the chair, a stranger with white hair and a benign smile.

"Nice idea, this," he said. "A lot of us old folks could do with more of these around the town. You know how many people there are here in Victoria with arthritis and bad hearts and the like? And not all of them that old either. Too many! This chair yours?"

"Kind of," she said. "A gift."

"Then this is probably yours too." He handed her an envelope and then got up to walk away. "Always feel down the sides of chairs. You'd be surprised."

★★★

Back in her own place, Althea opened the envelope slowly.

She counted the bills slowly.

She multiplied a hundred by fifty slowly.

Where had the old lady got all these lovely brown notes? Five thousand dollars worth.

She fanned them out and held them up to the light. Hardly likely that Mrs. K. was into money laundering or forgery. They had to be real.

It was common for old people to keep cash around because they couldn't get out to the bank often. Usually they hid it in the most likely places for a burglar to look. There was no name on the envelope and as she'd said to the elderly stranger, the chair was a gift. She was its owner.

Her thoughts began to run on diverging tracks: the chair was given to me. Whatever was in it is mine. The chair belonged to Mrs. K. who possibly intended the money for her daughter. But then Mrs. K. didn't intend to die so soon and this was probably her contingency fund. On the finders-keepers theory, the money belonged to the old man who had left no address and was long gone. Or was he a fairy godfather who knew of her problem and had brought the money to her – a kind of fantasy Fedex. On that basis it was definitely hers. A truly intended gift. Her mother had said often enough that you don't look a gift horse in the mouth, though she had never been sure what was referred to. There hadn't been a lot of either gifts or horses around in those years.

★★★

Althea made herself a cup of coffee and kept on thinking. She could have called Sam about the money but he would have wanted a share. She could have gone to see her Dad in the hospital and waited for a sign from him but he had been out of it for a year or more. If she'd been religious she might have gone to church but any Holy Father would have told her to give the money to the poor. She could pay two months' rent, buy a smart new outfit to go job-hunting in and still have a couple of thousand left to put in the bank.

If, however, the money was not meant to be hers, then the Fates might strike at her for taking it. Sanjeet and his I Ching could have come in handy.

One small corner of her conscience was telling her that the money belonged to Martina. But did Martina need it? Was need the criterion? She looked at the now empty envelope and at the bills spread out on the table.

The phone rang. This was the sign. This call would in some way tell her whether to take the money and run or hand it over to its rightful owner.

It was Martina.

"Althea?"

Who else did she expect? Had she already found out about the cash?

"Martina?"

"I forgot to ask for your key."

"Oh right. I'll leave it in the manager's office tomorrow."

"Thank you."

There was a pause in which Althea could have said, "I have something of yours," or Martina might make a friendly remark. Neither of them spoke. And then Martina repeated her "Thank you." And Althea said, "Fine." It was a game to see which of them would hang up first. Althea waited and when she heard the buzz of the dead line, knew what she had to do.

She went downstairs and took the sign off the rocker, pushed it back to the elevator and rode with it to her floor. She picked up the envelope, tucked five of the hundred dollar bills into it and pushed it down the side of the cushion. Then she took the chair up to Mrs. K.'s apartment, opened the door one last time with her key and pushed the chair inside.

III

It was the custom in those days to treat all guests as royalty, even the beggar who turned up at the gate in rags. To honour the gods, the host, however poor he might be, would give the visitor food and wine from his table, not bones and scraps, but the best parts of the joint. Dire things could happen to a man or woman who turned away a stranger or denied him food and a night's lodging: the gods had a sneaky way of turning up in rags, disguised as homeless wanderers. And then the king himself . . .

After she'd told the kids the story of Odysseus's return home which they liked because of the bloody ending, Althea asked them what they would give to a homeless person who turned up at the house poor and badly dressed. She told them to think carefully about their answers. They were to give something that was precious to them.

"I'd let the guy check his email on my computer," Ricky said.

There was derisive laughter from the others.

"That's a good answer," Althea said. "Ricky probably doesn't like people to use his computer. That would be hard for him to do. Come on, you others."

John said slowly, "I would give him my hockey sweater."

From Sean, the mythical guest received all the ice cream in the fridge.

"What if it's a woman?" Joel asked.

"They eat ice cream."

"I mean," Joel said, "she might like something of my mom's. And my mom might not want to give her a coat or a dress."

"You must have something you could give her."

Joel thought and said, "OK. She can have my duvet to keep her warm."

Carter near to tears offered his dog, Lucky.

Thomas, his arms across his chest, said, "My dad says we have to be careful of strangers."

"I think we can make a story out of this," Althea said. "Think about it and next time we'll put it all together. Where does the stranger come from? Where will he or she go? What will he do with your gifts?"

"Sell them," Thomas shouted. "It's what they do. They pretend to be poor and they get things and sell them."

"You've got a week," she said. "Enjoy Spring Break."

"We're going to Disney World," Sean said.

"I have to go to my Gran's so *they* can go to work," John said.

It was still light and none of the boys lived more than five blocks away. Althea watched them walking down the road, straggling, pushing each other, arguing. Only Joel and Ricky would think the thing through and come back with ideas. She was treading on dangerous ground again. She'd been fired for trying to get her grade three class to think. Wasn't that part of true education? The principal said the problem was the subject she'd asked them to think about. Three parents had complained. Only three out of twenty-two seemed like a pretty good success rate to Althea. Confronting the most vocal of them, though, hadn't been a smart thing to do.

And so far, nine months later, there was still no regular job in sight. The tepid tone of the principal's reference letter was causing prospective employers to look at her without enthusiasm. She was 'reliable', meaning only that she turned up on time.

***

The boys' parents paid her to keep their boys off the street after school on Mondays, Wednesdays and Fridays. That brought in two hundred and seventy dollars a week. Research for the author who was writing a book on the history of Vancouver Island took a lot of time for little pay but the book was almost done. With her E.I. she had just enough for the rent, the car payments, the dentist, the phone and food.

The money she'd come to think of as Mrs. Kraznowski's legacy was long gone. As was her apartment in that building. This rented studio, a fancy name for a room with a Murphy bed plus minute kitchen and bathroom, wouldn't be hers for long either. The owner wanted to take over the whole house and turn it into a bed and breakfast. In summer he could make more in three months on that space than she would pay him in a year.

***

Her classes with the boys had come about by chance. She'd met one of the parents in the supermarket and he remembered her from school. He had liked her, approved of what she was trying to do, was sorry she'd had to leave. Ricky was still having trouble with his reading due, his dad said, to lack of stimulation. Would she help? One boy became two and then three and she'd drawn the line at six. She read to them. They read to her. They talked. It was two hours of dealing with words. And it left her exhausted.

After she'd seen the boys out and washed their glasses and cleaned up the cookie crumbs, she sat down to do a life-check.

I am thirty-one. I have an unattractive reference letter from a school where I taught for four terms. Only one senior citizen is on my visiting list. Sam has moved to the mainland, seeing it as more profitable and a better source of his drug of choice: Sex. My mother has moved to Australia with her new lover. That last was only a wish. Her mother called from Alberta every three days to tell her to get a fulltime job and/or find a man.

I'm looking, Mom!

A new hotel twenty storeys high had opened downtown. Surely in the huge local hospitality industry, there was a place for a cheerful woman with teaching skills and a way with old people.

She decided to keep a diary of her efforts so that if she died in the attempt it could be sent to her mother to show that she truly had tried.

***

Monday: Wearing the dark brown pantsuit and cream shirt bought with the 'legacy', I went to the Right- for-You employment agency. (I got the name from the Yellow Pages.) A receptionist took down my details and told me to return on . . .

Tuesday: Wearing the same outfit, I turned up smiling for my appointment with a Ms. Jeanne Poiret. Do you speak French? Not in a way that anyone can understand. Pity. But perhaps . . .

Wednesday: All smiles, Ms. Poiret told me she had something I might like. She passed a piece of paper across the table. You have to be kidding, I said. She said, You can't be too choosy at your age and with your skills. Told her to try again.

Thursday: Stayed home. Argued with owner of house about loud music. It's my consolation, I said. Get off your ass, he replied. Plugged in earphones.

Friday: Call from Ms. Poiret. Trying to get hold of you yesterday. Something a little out of the ordinary. Might just suit you. Should I be flattered? Or insulted? As it turned out . . .

***

It was one of the large old stone houses that were built by British soldiers or civil servants retiring from long stints in India or Africa at the end of the nineteenth century. There were shabby but beautiful rugs on the hall floor and weapons, swords and spears, hanging on the walls. Nothing had been dusted in a while. Althea hoped she hadn't been hired to clean.

Monday morning, I turned up at the address Ms. Poiret had given me and was taken in (odd choice of words) by a woman in a nurses' outfit, the kind they wear now. Flowered top. Blue pants. Standard issue.

I am without a lover at the moment.

The nurse asked her to wait there in the hall.

Althea waited. After five or ten minutes, a door opened and a good deal of noise and a woman came through it.

"Ms. McCormac?"

"Yes. Ms. Groman?

"That's right. I'm Meredith Groman. Come right in. Do sit down."

Althea went in and sat on the edge of a large armchair and tried to look efficient but it was difficult because pictures of men and women, singly and in groups, were projected intermittently on the end wall and loud music was bouncing off the ceiling. She couldn't pick out the words but it sounded like the theme song of an old musical.

Ms. Groman pulled a remote control device out of her pocket and magically the pictures stood still and the music stopped. It was a relief.

"Tell me about yourself."

I'm without a lover at the moment.

"I'm looking for a change. I have a degree in."

"Yes. Yes. Yes. But why are you here this morning?"

The phrases Althea had put together on the way fled from her mind. This woman demanded honesty. "I need a job."

"What I need is – well it's too grand actually to say an archivist – but my papers and books need cataloguing and packing. I can get the videos edited in time, I think. But it's the labelling. I'm going to die you see. We all are, I know. But I probably won't see Christmas. So I can't do with wasting time."

Althea wanted to cry or to take the woman in her arms and tell her it wasn't true. Ms. Groman was not a wraith, not a pale shadow. She was tall and well-built, fiftyish, and her complexion was – on closer look – artificial.

"I'm very sorry," was all Althea could think of to say.

"Don't be. When you think about it, you could be killed on your way home by a drunk driver. At least I know my time has come."

"What do you do? I mean why the archive?"

"Good. That's the right question. I'm a documentary maker. You won't have seen my work. I'll explain. During the war in England there was something called Mass Observation. People were employed to go about the streets, air raid shelters, pubs, wherever and listen to what was being said. It gave the government a good idea of morale, of how the population was bearing up under the tremendous stress. It seems to me that this is also a stressful time and so. So, Ms. McCormac, I haven't got words to waste. I need my notes and recordings put in order. It's a documentary. Something that may be important only to me. On the other hand, it might go far. What do you think?"

"Yes," Althea said. "My name's Althea."

"You can start tomorrow at 9?"

"Yes."

"Good. The woman who let you in is here to give me an injection. She comes twice a week. I live here with my father and we have a housekeeper who's here every day except Sunday."

And that was that. She had never been hired so quickly. Fired quickly, yes. But taken on without a look at the questionable reference? That woman had courage. She'd accepted the word of a stranger who might, for all she knew, be the look-out for a gang of burglars.

On the way home, Althea realised that she hadn't asked Ms. Groman about the pay. About hours. About benefits. She hadn't questioned her new employer's bona fides either. But she didn't care. A quick moment of trust, a little current, had run between them. She wanted to help this strange and tragic woman and to stay with her to the very end. The housekeeper would surely give her lunch on working days. If necessary, she could sleep at the Y or, at the absolute worst, beg from her mother. She was filled with the knowledge that this was something she was meant to do. Sam, when she called and told him, would understand.

She foresaw late evenings on the job and left messages for the parents, apologising for the short notice, to tell them there would be no more classes after today. If at some future time . . .

★★★

All six boys turned up as usual after school. Joel and Ricky brought out a folded sheet on which they had written every item that they or the people they knew might give to a beggar at their doors. Carter was late because he had gone home to fetch Lucky. Some instinct had told him that Althea was the needy person and that he should make his sacrifice to her. She would have liked to give him a hug but that was out of the question in these cold times.

When they'd drunk their juice and eaten the chocolate cake she'd bought specially, Althea told them she was sorry this was to be their last meeting. Carter was happy to be taking his pet home with him. Sean told her it had been great. On his way out, as a parting shot, Thomas said, "It's been OK coming here but my dad says you've been giving us ideas."

★★★

Althea poured herself a glass of Chardonnay from the bottle she'd bought on her way home from the Groman house. Her life, she figured, would go on like this and she was not discontented. It would be a matter of fits and starts. Her jobs might always be short-term but she had her effect. For the rest of their lives, the boys would remember Odysseus and the beggar at the gates. Mrs. Kraznowski had enjoyed her company in her last months. Sam had loved her for a little while. You have no staying power, her mother often said. But was that a virtue, staying power? There was always a need for someone to fill the gaps left by those who stayed and then fell by the wayside.

She pressed the cream shirt and sorted out her clothes for morning. She left a note for the landlord and gave him a month's notice.

It only took me a week to find a job, mother. The man might take longer.

IV

Carols seeped through the walls of the store, stopping only when a voice broke in to warn customers that a mere fifteen days remained to Christmas.

Martina hadn't noticed Althea standing near her in the women's wear department at The Bay until she spoke. Althea had a black jacket in her hand and Martina couldn't help wondering if she intended to steal it.

"You look as if you've been away," was how Althea greeted her.

Martina's instinct was to back off, dart behind the rack of long gowns and pretend she hadn't heard. But it wasn't as though the woman could come back into her life. She had no need for sympathy now, her life was just fine thank you very much. Almost fine. So she smiled and said, "Hello, Althea. It's been a while."

"How have you been?"

"I'm just back from my honeymoon."

"Congratulations."

“And you. What are you up to now?”

“My employer died last week.”

Althea looked close to tears. This is a mistake, Martina told herself even as she said aloud, “Come and have coffee.”

What she saw in the shape of this woman she had disliked was a loser, a pathetic sort of person who only knew how to manage her life by latching on to others. In a sense she was a leech. And yet she had been kind to her mother when she herself had found it difficult.

The café was tucked into a corner of the store. Althea ordered a cappuccino and insisted on paying for them both.

“You were going to buy the black jacket?”

“For the funeral.”

“Was he very old?”

“She. Fifty-one. Cancer.”

“I’m sorry.”

“She was a wonderful woman. We were . . . ” The tears began to roll.

“You’d become friends?”

“She was. I’d never known anyone like her, you see. Generous and – and creative.”

Martina gave her a few moments to recover, moments in which she looked for an escape route, then she asked, “What will you do now?”

“There are loose ends.”

Out of work, stranded. Hopeless!

“Althea, by the way, I’m really sorry about the chair. I knew you didn’t want it really.” Oh God! Why had she let those words out? Why had she admitted to such awful behaviour instead of just letting it go? “Look. Something’s been on my mind all these months. I’m going to write you a cheque. There was an envelope down the side of the chair. It should have been yours. I gave the chair to you.”

"No. No." Althea was looking at her as if she were an alien or had offered her a dead fish.

Martina, wishing she'd kept her mouth shut, said, "I'd like you to have it."

She wrote Althea McCormac and the amount and the date and signed her name and handed the cheque across the table.

"Well. That's a surprise. Thank you. If you're sure."

"I'm sure."

* * *

"You married the guy who was in Manila? Ron, the businessman?"

Of course, her mother had talked to Althea in those months. She knew everything.

"No. I married Harry, my boss. We've just come back from Greece."

"Greece. I've always wanted to go there. Was it wonderful?"

How to answer that? Harry had got an infected blister. She had suffered from diarrhoea. They'd quarrelled. She'd even considered walking away.

"We had a great time."

"The Acropolis by moonlight?"

The conversation was going the way of a bad play. Martina put the cheque book in her purse and closed it.

"I have to be getting back," she said and then, was it guilt that was driving her for goodness sake! she couldn't stop herself from going on, "This is my new address. Come and see us. We're having a housewarming on Sunday at three."

"I'd love to."

"See you there."

Althea said, "It's funny, you never know whether you're going to be a beggar at the gates or a guest at the table. It's all in the lap of the gods."

"I guess." Martina hurried away. Althea was a strange, disturbing person. Not settled. She was a woman who bounced around the edges, making a mockery of the straightforward. Why was she was allowing her back into her life, into her house? She could call and tell her the party was off. But she had no idea where Althea lived.

Althea sat on in the café. There was no need to hurry. Meredith had instructed her lawyer to pay her and to allow her to stay on in the house until she had finished the archive. It was going to take a while. She stared at the piece of paper in her hand and laughed. Then she got up and went to the china department to buy a gift to take with her on Sunday, a nice bowl perhaps that cost exactly the amount of the cheque generous Martina had written: a hundred and fifty dollars.

V

Married. I am *married*, Martina was saying to herself. There was her *husband* handing drinks to the people from the office. I am married to Harry. On the third day of their honeymoon she had seen his paunchy silhouette against the window and understood what she had done. She had *committed* herself. This new house, striking in its bold colours and modern design, was part of the deal. Harry. House. Home? Had she scored a home run?

She went to greet her brother and Hanna and the little girls. Her family and friends were now witnesses to the deed. All of them bore gifts to seal the deal. She said thank you to Robert for the second package he put into her hands. Hanna pulled her to one side and said, "Don't open it now. It's the tank. We don't allow war toys."

Martina had found the tank when she was moving and

wrapped it to send to her nieces for Christmas. These nosy parents obviously peeked into their kids' gifts ahead of time. Well screw them! Had their aversion to guns and killing machines ever saved a single life?

She let them move on toward Harry who was being *jovial.* Congratulations filled the room, a swarm of bees, although there were no more than fifteen people in it. The buzz in the air murmured: *This is your place. You have come into your kingdom.* These people couldn't know that she was having doubts about the king. She took a deep breath and made an effort to improve her mood.

"Martina?"

It was Althea tentatively crossing the threshold holding a huge package, her offering to the household gods.

"I'm so glad you could come," Martina said, taking the gift, weighed down by it.

"It's good of you to invite me."

"You didn't have to bring anything. But thank you."

"I couldn't come to a new house without, you know, a present."

Althea was wearing a silky skirt and a Chinese jacket. She looked splendid, assured, almost rich. She would be a stranger to all these people. But she was an invited guest and must be treated kindly and introduced – as 'My friend Althea'?

She chose to say to her brother, "This is Althea McCormac, mother's friend."

As she went to greet another newcomer, she heard Harry shout across the room, "Althea! Come and have a drink."

He knew her! Harry, her new husband, knew the woman, was *acquainted* with her. Later she would ask. Now she turned to watch as they hugged each other like old lovers.

"Martina," Harry said. "Come and meet Althea."

"We've met," Althea said. "I knew Mrs. Kraznowski."

"Amazing. You never mentioned her, Marti. We go way back, me and Althea. This is great. It's been years." He introduced her to the others, an old friend lost and re-discovered.

Martina served food and drink and smiled till she felt as if her teeth had receded into her gums. She accepted compliments about the house. *Lucky to find it. Such a view. Great garden.* No one commented on the furniture which was an inharmonious mixture of his and hers. Country music, Harry's choice, provided a background to the chat. Mozart, he said, was not to be used as a gap-filler for when conversation slowed. She picked out a line: 'the sound of the speed of loneliness.' Could that be it? Had she accepted Harry on the third time of asking because she heard loneliness quickly approaching? She shuddered and then formed her lips into a smile again.

★★★

The guests did eventually leave and she stood beside her husband to survey the mess.

"This big package from Althea," he said. "Why don't you open it."

Martina unwrapped it slowly, almost afraid. It was a lovely ceramic bowl, the kind to use for pasta at a party.

"Generous," Harry said. "She left the price tag on."

Martina looked and saw the amount. Althea knew? Did Althea know that there had been more cash in that envelope? Perhaps she had counted the money and then put all those notes back into the envelope, stuffed it back down the side of the chair and returned the damn thing. She had behaved totally honestly. Martina felt criminal. She had made out that she was doing a good deed and had been caught cheating. She wanted to throw up.

"Funny seeing Althea again," Harry was saying. "I knew her when she was working part-time in the library. She'd just come out here from Alberta. A kid really. Looking for a job. She was kind to me after my Dad died. You don't need to look at me like that. So yes. We had a bit of an affair. Then we lost touch." He put his arm round Martina, drawing her close. "You're a bit alike in some ways. Two of a kind. But I like you best."

Martina was still picturing Althea putting the money back into the envelope.

"She's sly," she said.

"Like I said," Harry replied. "You're two of a kind. We'll invite her over for dinner. I'll make Fettuccine Alfredo."

Martina looked at him. He was a gregarious, pleasing man. A man who had apparently admired her for years. He could cook and make salad. He put his arm round her in a comforting and gentle way. She leaned into his embrace. "I don't know where she lives," she said.

"She wrote her address in the book," Harry answered.

And Martina knew that unless she went out one dark night and did the woman in, she was stuck with Althea for life.

Ice

THE SNOW HAD BEGUN TO BLOW AROUND and he could see no further than the dog's kennel in the yard outside. School had been out for fifteen minutes. In weather like this, all the kids knew to go straight home. So where was Mary? It was only a five-minute walk. Maybe a couple of minutes more against the wind. Brian began to pull on his caribou pants. She could have fallen and would soon be hypothermic, soon freeze. At least Jeffie, home with an upset stomach, was safe indoors. He fastened his jacket and pulled the hood over his woollen cap and pushed his hands into his mitts, glad he'd chosen today to work from home.

When he opened the outer door, the wind slammed at his face and iced his moustache. Conal, whimpering, followed him to the length of the chain as if advising him not to go. "All right, boy," he said, and the dog went back to his kennel. The school was a dim shape over the road beyond the igloo-shaped church.

Why did we have to come to this godforsaken place? Shannon had asked that a thousand times. Why do you stay? And now she was in Montreal, begging him to send their son to 'civilization', telling Brian to follow at the end of the year, vowing never to return to live with him in Iqaluit. *If you love me, if you still love me.* He had no reply to that. If he opened his mouth to call out, it would fill with cold and besides she wouldn't hear against the wind.

Yesterday a bear had been seen near the school. *Ursus maritimus.* According to the age-old tales, *nanuk* could change into a man at will. And change back. Man to bear. Who knew which was the primary shape or what the intentions were of beast or human? His jacket and pants were white with snow. What kind of a frightening figure was he, himself? *It's only Daddy, Mary.*

There were no human shapes in the schoolyard. No children to be seen making their way home. He reached the door. The principal was locking up and about to leave. They nodded to each other, she waved her hand to show that the school was empty and Brian watched her struggle on past the climbing frame towards her house. He was being foolish. Mary had gone to Lukassie's or to Susie's. She was too smart not to take shelter. Even now at home, the phone would be ringing. Jeffie would say, "Dad? I dunno. I think he went out." Mary would worry in her turn. It was circular. Whoever was out in the storm had to be accounted for, and quickly. The freezing cold was a killing force, a challenge. Only those who knew how to deal with it, how to withstand its violence, should be allowed to stay. This country belonged to the Inuit who understood it. It was a land for heroes, for survivors, not for soft people from the South.

I don't understand. That was Shannon's voice again. He could get work elsewhere. Anywhere. "We do not belong," she had said often enough. "We are intruders. The Island is hostile to us." He had explained that there was work to do, to help the people help themselves in their transition to a different way of life. "Is it what they want?" she had shouted, accusing him of arrogance, of colonialism. She had always refused to eat *muktuk*. And besides. And besides.

She should know that he couldn't leave while there were mysteries to solve. The more the land tried to drive him out, the more he had to stay to warn people of the early melt. It was his responsibility.

The animal skins he was wearing couldn't keep the cold from his lungs. His feet were chilled and every step was an effort. His eyes stung. He covered his mouth with his mitten and walked in short diagonals to cover the widest area. Unless he went back and completed the diamonds and then made a line up the middle of them, he could miss his child. Her cold body might be two feet away and he wouldn't know. Mary, thirteen years old, bright and affectionate, his laughing girl, loved to go out on the skidoo with him, liked to test her strength against this harsh landscape. He should have brought the *komatik* to pull her back home. The street was invisible. But she must be in the house by now. He had to get back and make hot chocolate. Sitting by the fire with a mug between her hands, she would thaw, she would smile. Then he saw her, saw Mary, and held out his arms to her. She was laughing, walking towards him, but when he tried to embrace her, she vanished. She was a shadow, a thin shadow that melted between his hands like ice.

★★★

Ice! His paper on the behaviour of ice still needed work. He took pictures of ice, measured it, studied it. It was not his department, not his area, they said, but it was what he had to do. He read about the way it broke up on the sea and watched the way it moved on the water in July when the ice-breaker came. He had the violent cracking, crunching sound of it on tape. He examined the shifting colours of blue and green and was in awe of its power, hated its unreliability. 'Terrible beauty,' that's what an Antarctic explorer had said about ice. And now it was beginning to recede, to melt earlier and earlier. That's what he had to make clear.

Shannon had gone along with his 'obsession' when they still shared loving, sorrowful days. But after she found that he was going out at all hours to check the changing formations of the ice in different conditions and planned to go further north to study a great iceberg, she said he'd gone crazy. But he was not crazy. He was simply searching – searching through the shaded layers for a truth. Because if he had only known . . .

Tonight there is caribou stew for dinner, honey. I made it this morning, enough for three days. With a loaf of his home-made bread it would be a feast for the three of them. Later they would play Scrabble and Jeffie would complain that it wasn't fair because the other two knew more words than he did.

The wind was pushing at him. He was going two steps forward and one step back. Nothing for it but to plod on. Just a few metres more.

I manage the house and keep my job at the Department of Housing and Infrastructure. I can do it. I do the research in my spare time. He was writing his own résumé in his head as if he wanted to apply for a position as husband to a busy woman! Are you out there? Are you a woman who would be glad of a man like me? I'm versatile. Ice is mysterious. You would have to agree to that one fact. And I know how to build an igloo. We will always be warm, Mary.

He could hear his own father murmuring, murmuring, "What are you doing there, so far away?" *Far away is the best place for me, Dad. And hardly anywhere is further away than this.*

He turned towards the light. *My feet are very cold.* Ice is made of crystals. An iceberg the size of Belgium is afloat in Antarctica. Titanically speaking, ice is a calamity. He laughed at his own joke and the intake of air hurt his throat.

The creature that loomed up in front of him was huge. "No," he said. As if it might understand English. "Get away from me, *nanuk*," he ordered and held up his hands to ward the beast off. But it spoke softly. "Lie down and rest," it said. "You'll feel better, Brian, if you sleep. Take off that heavy jacket, Brian, my love, my sweet." So Karen his first love was here. They were lying beside the lake in Muskoka. Her voice was gentle as honey. Her sharp fingers grabbing at the edges of his coat tried to pull the hood from his head.

"Karen," he said, "you must understand that the answers are important to you as well as to me, and to the world. The entire world. And the world is not a paperweight."

The music was soft and romantic. He was ready to dance. But there was no floor. Smoothly he glided around, holding the hand of his partner. They were airborne. It was beautiful. The universe was a bright place. He was looking down on it. The castle on the hill was where they lived. Where they all lived. Loving people were passing him one to another as if he were a child, admiring him.

"Is he there? Is he in there?"

The question was strange.

"I don't know," he replied.

"We got to him just in time," they said, whoever they were.

Whoever he was.

★★★

Shannon was looking at him. There were tears in her eyes. He wasn't sure why she was standing over him, or why he was lying down.

"Why did you go out?" she asked.

There is fast ice and sea ice. Glacial ice melted is good for brewing tea on a camping trip.

You have to consider the katabatic winds.

"The storm," was all he could think of to say.

"You left Jeffie alone."

"Mary."

Shannon sat in the chair by the bed, her back to him.

He was in bed. It was not his room or his house. There was a cage over his legs.

"Did you have to?" she asked.

The swirling thoughts in his mind settled down.

"I'm feeling my way out of this," he answered. Pain made him cry out.

His memory returned as his brain thawed. He knew with awful clarity what his wife was about to say and allowed her words to hit him like pellets of frozen rain.

"Mary died playing with her friends on the shore six months ago. In the Bay. The ice closed over her. You couldn't get to her in time. It was not your fault, Brian."

"If I'd known more about the melt I could have told her to stay off it."

Patiently she said as if for the fiftieth time, "There was nothing you could have done."

She'd brought him a portable CD player and a number of discs. He looked through them and was grateful that it was a collection of classical works by Beethoven and Vivaldi and that there was nothing by Mahler nor any of the music they'd enjoyed together twenty years ago.

"Thank you," he said because she'd understood that he wasn't up to romantic memories.

"We'll talk about the future when you're on your – on your way to being better. Jeffie is here now."

"Here?"

"Montreal. They medevacked you. Your boss put Jeffie on the plane yesterday."

After Shannon had gone, Brian tried to move his toes. The left ones responded. The right ones were still frozen. There was no connection. No connection at all. They should bring him a heating pad.

So the day before yesterday he had gone out on a stormy afternoon to find a daughter who would never come back. What or who had impelled him, drawn him out into the murderous cold? Was there a vengeful spirit out there who wanted a life for a life? Or was Mary calling from the depths for her father to come and join her?

★★★

"Un pied nouveau. A prosthetic foot," the doctor was saying. "You'll never have arthritic toes or corns. It'll be the same size. Your shoes will fit. On peut danser."

The nurse was standing behind the doctor, waiting perhaps to hold Brian's hand as he wept for his right foot or to offer him a pill for shock or even to put her arms round him and tell him he was lucky not to have lost his whole leg.

"I wasn't a good dancer before," he said. "Maybe I'll be able to tango now."

Both of them smiled at him, relieved that he wasn't going to shriek and make a fuss. The doctor patted his shoulder; he was a brave patient. He smiled back and watched them walk out of the room. If he had a meltdown later, it would not be on their watch.

There were flowers on the locker, the cards on the shelf. People knew what had happened. The wind from the North was carrying the whispers of his friends and colleagues to him: *He went out to look for his daughter. He's nuts. He couldn't get over her death. He forgot to put his boots on.*

★★★

His foot was perhaps a sacrifice that had to be made? The sharp-fingered spectre who had taken off his hood and undone his jacket had known that the spirits of the place must be placated. Sedna kept his daughter imprisoned in her fishy kingdom.

Mary under the sea was combing the locks of the demanding goddess.

A young volunteer pushing a trolley brought him juice in a styrofoam cup. She smiled at him with palpable pity. As she went out, she turned and gave him a rueful look as if she wished she could help him but could think of nothing to say. He was a man in his prime and this girl was looking at him as if he was old and finished.

He looked at the cup, heard the wheels of the trolley move down the corridor, imagined the slim girl pushing it along and smiling at each patient in turn. He began to cry and he cried as if an ice jam had broken up to let the water through. Words spun through his head in no sensible order. *Terror. Chill. Nanuk. Child. Jeffie. Warmth. Blue. Green. Beauty.* He pulled the sheet up over his face so that he couldn't be seen.

The world of ice was not his world. It had rejected him. The myths were not his myths, they belonged to the people who'd inhabited that land for thousands of years. *Did you have to do that?* His Dad speaking again on the summer day when he'd swum out to the island and had to be brought back by boat. *What were you trying to prove?*

***

"You're going to need a few weeks of rehab." Shannon's voice came to him through the bedclothes.

He put his head out and let her see his ravaged face.

"You won't be going back there?"

Like the spirit in the storm she spoke gently. Like the spirit, she wanted to mislead him.

"There'll be a job for you in Ottawa. And I can teach there." She was offering him a chance to enjoy an easier life, to be a husband, to have, if it was possible with only one foot, sex with her again. He couldn't help laughing as he imagined taking off his clothes, her clothes, and then removing a plastic and metal device from the end of his leg before he climbed into bed.

She patted his hand, seeing hysteria. “So you’ll stay, love.”

He heard her talking about getting the furniture brought South by sea in the summer. Papers, books, a few clothes, could be put on a plane. She would return to Iqaluit herself to make the arrangements.

“Yes,” he said. There was no need for her to know that he wasn’t responding to her but to the voice of the tundra.

Summer Romance

JENNIFER SAID, "YOU ARE LUCKY. You'll learn so much from him." And Fran agreed. She packed her shorts and swimsuit and her tennis racquet and her laptop and set out prepared for almost anything. Of all the summer jobs going, this was the prize. Living with the writer in his lakeshore place. Work in the mornings. Swimming in the afternoons. Wine and literary gossip in the evenings. Though she did plan to cut down on alcohol. There'd been too many days lately when her head felt like a pumpkin with somebody in there scraping the seeds out. *I will be healthy!*

Her mother's goodbye at the bus station, "I'm going to grit my teeth and make the marriage work," was enough to make her want to walk to Muskoka if there'd been no other way to get there. She climbed onto the bus quickly and was glad of the darkened window.

The bus made its way towards forest and peace through thick traffic, dense streets, industrial 'parks'. Left in her wake were her friends, her parents' arguments and, thank God, James and his demands. Freedom and fir trees and proximity to fame lay ahead. Three months of summer days – and nights. She would become indispensable to the great man. She would shyly confess her own writing ambitions. He would endorse her first book. In the front of his next he would write, *without her valuable assistance . . .* He might fall in love with her but she would have to refuse him gently on the moonlit beach out of sight of the cottage and his wife. He would be understanding but might cry a little. There would be no 'reader, she married him' ending to this story. She got out her iPod and spent the rest of the journey listening to *Genesis*.

A taxi driver at the bus depot in Huntsville asked for her by name. She handed him her suitcase and backpack. Steven Arndt was going to treat her well. In the back seat, she waved a queenly hand to the firs and the slim birches and sighed with pleasure as the car left the road and drove along a lane to a rocky point jutting out into the lake. The cottage stood alone, a private place.

"Isolated," the driver said. "Strange people. Him and her. But they spend money in town. So! Have yourself a good summer."

★★★

The cottage door was open. Fran called hello and looked inside and called again. There was no response. She turned and saw the cloud of dust raised by the taxi as it drove away. In front of her the lake was smooth. Other cottages were dotted in the trees across the inlet, well out of shouting distance. There was no sign of a boat out on the water or anyone swimming. Round the back of the building stood a car covered in pine needles, and a bicycle. A canoe was propped up against the wall. The sun had gone in. It was the solstice. Standing there, Fran felt like an intruder in a Tom Thomson painting as if she might forever remain among these trees beside the lake late on a summer evening: June 21st 2005.

★★★

At least she could help herself to a glass of water. The kitchen was ramshackle as if no one cared much about food. It smelled of fish. The fridge was full of bottles, wine and Evian water. She hesitated to put a glass under the tap.

There were five rooms on the ground floor. One was obviously his study: his five books on well-known Canadian writers and literary theory were displayed on a low shelf. His recent novel stood on a lectern, open. Did he read it every day as if it were a bible? *In the beginning were my words!* He'd gone in for fiction, he told an interviewer, because there was a dearth of well-written stories; the computer in this modern age had replaced imagination. The desk was a slab of wood set on trestles. A page of handwriting lay on top of a pile of paper. She backed out of the shrine.

The living room was barely furnished with beat-up couches and a TV set. In the small dining room, a table was set for one. The two bedrooms looked unoccupied. Fran assumed that one of them was for her. She didn't go upstairs but decided to sit outside and wait. After all, he was expecting her. Who had sent the taxi to meet her if not him or his wife?

She didn't want to cry. Too old for that. But she had expected to be greeted, to be offered food and drink. On the other hand, perhaps some disaster had struck and the Arndts had rushed to the hospital in their other car. If they had another car. Maybe she had come on the wrong day. But the taxi! Maybe the writer had swum too far out and drowned, taking her dream job with him.

It was getting dark and the branches were rustling. A bird cried a warning sound. An animal pattered by. She went into the cottage and closed the door.

I arrived at the cottage to be greeted by – no one. The phone. There was a phone. But who to call?

She went back to the study. The page of handwriting that she had assumed to be part of a manuscript might be a clue, even a letter addressed to her. But there was no 'Dear Francesca' or 'Dear Ms. Giancarlo' written at the top. She read. She stood there and re-read.

I chose a moment when no one was around. It didn't take long. There wasn't much blood. We live alone all summer at the edge of a lake and no one will know at what hour or on what day she disappeared. There will eventually have to be an explanation but for a couple of months I'll be free to enjoy the company of . . .

"Aha!"

She turned. And there he was. He was taller than her Dad who was six two, and broader across the shoulders. Dark curly hair and beard. Sharp nose, wide mouth. A living breathing copy of the picture on his book covers.

She shrank back from him and then moved forward smiling. She wasn't a gothic heroine and this man was not a monster. He was a fiction writer. He made things up.

"Do you always snoop around, Ms. Giancarlo? Assuming you are she."

"I thought it might be a note. I've been here a while."

"I had to go to North Bay. Back later than I thought. You must be tired. Your bedroom is the one on the left next to the bathroom."

Fran decided to get their relationship off on the right foot.

"I'm hungry," she said.

"I've brought fresh bread, and cheese. Help yourself. I'll see you in the morning."

***

He was not very polite, she thought, but it was after midnight. She made herself a cheese sandwich and ate it quickly. The light was dim and there was an eerie feeling to the place as if someone had died there recently. In the small bedroom she didn't bother to unpack but undressed and lay down on the bed, tossing around, thinking, listening. Something was gnawing at the cottage wall. Couldn't be him. If he wanted to rape her he had only to open the bedroom door. There was no need for him to chew through it. Must be a porcupine. Odd squeals echoed outside. Moments later she heard heavy breathing, definitely an intake of air and a long whistling kind of exhalation. Then uneven footsteps thumped around on the floor above and down the stairs. She sat up and reached for her tennis racquet. The feet stopped outside her door. The door was opened very slightly.

In a whisper, he said, "Are you awake?"

It was best to say yes. Then perhaps he would keep away.

"Yes," she said. She hadn't expected him to come on to her so soon.

"If you're too hot, there's a fan in the closet. Plug it into the outlet by the window."

The door closed again.

***

Morning did come. She had slept but at 5 a.m. birds were calling to each other. An outboard was revving up. She hoped that Mr. Arndt wouldn't expect too much from her on this first day.

She washed quietly and dressed and went into the kitchen. There appeared to be little in the way of breakfast food. No boxes of cereal, no eggs, no coffee. She cut slices off the loaf he'd brought back last night and made herself tea and toast and sat at the picnic table outside. It was chilly but the waves rippled on the rocks and there were no city sounds of sirens and impatient traffic. She walked around and then fetched her notebook and began to work on the story she'd started last week.

At ten o'clock when she felt ready to go back to sleep, Mr. Arndt came out to her and said, "Let me look at your hands."

He turned them over and asked, "Not used to heavy work?"

"You said you wanted a proof-reader and some help in the kitchen."

"Normally. But I need to move something heavy. I'm going to the coffee shop in town for breakfast. You've had something?

Good. Meanwhile, you can begin on the manuscript. Short stories. On the right. Look for typos. Spelling slips. I don't, DO NOT, want to hear what you think of my prose."

He went out.

He drove away.

She added *arrogant* to *ill-mannered.* This wasn't the kind of freedom she'd anticipated, the freedom to starve, to steal whatever there was in the cottage, to burn the place down if she chose. She was a stranger and yet he trusted her. That was odd to begin with. She was left here to read his manuscript and to answer the phone. She felt lonely and hungry and tired and she wanted a mug of coffee. She would even have talked to James. But Arndt was going to pay her well. That was the deal. And she was here to work.

She went into the study. The page she'd read the night before had gone. The proofs of his collection lay on the centre of the desk with a note on top that said, READ THIS. She felt like Alice.

She also felt like calling Professor Braeme, Helga, who had kindly arranged this job for her: 'It will expand your knowledge of English Literature. You need to get away from the old classics. Too much of them can warp your mind. He's an expert on the Post-Colonial.' *He is an expert in the art of making a person feel unwelcome.*

She began to read, pencil in hand, ready to mark any errors.

Page I

The Girl in the Trees. A borrowed title surely.

The girl was small, no higher than a piano. She was warfed by the birches.

Fran put a *d* in the margin and a caret by the word and sat in the easy chair by the window to read the whole story. Corrections could come later.

Ill at ease, the man watched as she walked in a Northerly direction and marked every third or fourth tree with a dab of paint from the pot she carried; a pot of dark green paint. The brush was made of badger hair as he discovered later when the paint was spilt over the ground and the girl.

***

"So it's a soporific?"

"Oh!" She'd been dreaming enjoyably of green dwarfs and badgers and came to, startled.

"My story."

"No. I didn't sleep well last night."

"Drink this coffee."

He was standing over her, looming in fact. Looming darkly. She took the cup and drank. It was bitter. Could be drugged. He hadn't even asked whether she liked coffee.

"We've got work to do, Francesca. Later you can tell me about yourself. We'll talk. If I seem offhand it's because I have problems."

He ceased to loom and moved to stand by the door.

"When you've drunk that, come outside."

Since it appeared she was to be a servant, she said, "Yes, Mr. Arndt," and after a few minutes she followed him and found him holding an axe.

"I want you to hold that end while I chop."

The end was attached to a thick rope wrapped round a box the size of a child's coffin that certainly hadn't been on the beach earlier. He'd made several knots in the rope and now wanted to cut the extra piece off.

"What's in here?" she asked.

"Stones," he said.

Or his wife in two pieces?

"I see."

"You don't see. We're going to take this out to the middle of the lake and push it overboard. How much do you weigh?"

"Fifty-five kilograms," she lied, losing four. Death by drowning. So soon?

"OK."

There was a boat with an outboard motor hidden in an inlet. He brought it round to the little beach and anchored it. Fran took a good look at the man's face. It was not a kind face. There was a driven, almost persecuted, look in his eyes. He was the sort of man who must have enemies.

But if he had killed his wife, he would surely not intend Fran to help with the disposal of body parts unless he planned to get rid of her too. Had she been brought here to be an accessory after the fact? *Last seen boarding a bus to Huntsville.*

Down, she said to her inner heroine.

"Verisimilitude," he said. "I'm writing about a man who drowns his girl friend in the lake. I want to know how the water looks, how it splashes, the sound it makes. What he might feel as the box goes down forever."

"Is your wife away?" she asked, meaning, is she dead? Meaning, are we to spend the entire summer here alone?

"She's not far away," he answered. "Come on now. Take your end."

The box wasn't as heavy as she'd expected, couldn't weigh more than forty kilos.

He steered the boat to where he said the lake was deepest and then cut the engine. Fran tried to admire the scenery.

"Now," he said. "We have to do this carefully. Don't want to fall in. Easiest to balance it on the side and let it go gently."

They managed to manoeuvre the box into position without standing up. The boat tipped to one side as they let go and water splashed over them as the 'coffin' and its contents disappeared into the lake. Arndt sat still for a while, silent. Then he said, "Ah. Good."

After lunch he told her that his wife had gone to Orillia to get treatment for her migraines but would be back soon. Meanwhile, there was a great deal to do.

They settled into a routine. He never invited her to go to the café with him for breakfast but allowed her to go to town in his car to buy food. At the end of the first week, she found herself telling him about James. James and his persistence. James wanting a serious relationship. Midway through the second week, she was describing her parents' fights and her distress.

Steven told her about the problems of living with a woman who had an almost permanent headache: he loved her but he was after all only a man.

***

Then it became the summer of her dreams. She wrote to Jennifer. *We sit on the steps and drink wine by moonlight. Sometimes we skinny-dip. I read proofs and file his papers and make simple meals. In the afternoons he works on his new novel, writing in longhand with a special pen. His wife has gone on from Orillia to visit her mother in Vancouver.*

On the second Friday, he made love to her. She let him see her stories and he said they showed great promise. She called home every week and wrote bland postcards to James.

Steven told her that in fact his wife had left in a fury because she said his novel was based on her and her first husband.

"Not true of course. Vain people always see themselves in works of fiction."

The word *idyll*, a word Fran associated with the colour green, was how she wanted to describe the passing days. She was drunk with the pungent smell of pine trees and the diesel fumes from power boats on the lake. She considered spending her life with him or at least going back to his place in Kingston for the coming winter. Far better, if she was to be a writer, to spend time listening and observing than going to school.

***

Ten days before Labour Day, Steven said to her, "It's over, honey. You'll have to leave on Wednesday. My wife has decided to forgive me."

"Will I see you again?" she asked.

"Let's not go there," he replied.

She dreaded returning home. Waiting to reclaim her was all the work she should have done. James was back from Europe wanting her to move in with him. Her friends were eager to know what it was like to live with the great Steven Arndt.

He was asleep but Fran didn't want to waste the remaining hours of this last night. The moon was shining through the thin blind on the window. She got out of bed quietly and went downstairs to have a look at the lake. And then she went into the study to imprint on her mind the place where they'd spent so much time together. The handwritten manuscript of his work-in-progress, the new novel, lay on the desk. She picked it up and flicked through the pages. *She is a tall girl with lovely young breasts and an unformed mind.* She read on. And on. It was all there, only the names were changed, everything she'd told him about James, about her parents, about her feelings. Little quotes from her stories were embedded in his text.

***

She went back to her own bedroom and spent the rest of the night dozing and thinking what a fool she'd been to trust such a man. How could she take revenge against a writer so highly regarded, so powerful?

At six o'clock she called a taxi. It would be better to sit around in the bus depot than spend one more hour in this place.

He came downstairs with a towel round his waist.

"Where are you going?"

"You're not a fiction writer at all," she yelled at him with all the anger she'd been storing through the dark hours. "You have no imagination. You're a fraud. You used me. Your wife is right."

He looked at her with scorn.

"You're just a little idiot. Come here."

"I'm leaving," she said.

He ran into his study and came back waving a sheet of paper as the taxi arrived.

"Sign this," he said.

She read it through; a promise not to discuss his work or their affair with anyone. She laughed, tore the sheet into pieces, climbed into the seat beside the driver and told him to step on it. The famous writer ran behind the car shouting and waving. His towel dropped to the ground. She wished she hadn't packed her camera. What a picture she could have emailed to her classmates.

"People always leave there in a hurry," the driver said. "Or they don't."

She walked around the depot and bought coffee and watched men and women come and go. She was very angry, with herself as much as with him. *You let him use you,* Jennifer would say. And she would be right. He had leeched off her, stolen the copyright of her life, taken it and would profit from it, get royalties on it.

She got on the bus and made her way to the back not wanting to talk to anyone. *Stupid idiot* was printed on her forehead. The book would come out. Her friends would read it. They would know. They would tell others. Everybody in Toronto, in Ontario, in Canada, the world, would know. James would know. Her parents, living in their tight-lipped truce, would have something new to argue about.

As they were drawing nearer to the smog, to the edges of the city, she thought about the handwritten page she'd read on her first night at the cottage. She shivered. If he always wrote from life then what exactly had she helped him to throw into the deepest part of the lake? There she had him! She would write a mystery set in that well-known spot and whether he had murdered his wife or not, whether he had gruesome intentions of any kind, didn't matter. Fiction would make it true.

The Magician's Beautiful Assistant

PAUL LAID THE DRESS DOWN ON THE BED. He straightened the folds and spread the skirt so that it flared and then he tucked in the waist. There were no sleeves and the bodice was cut low. He stood still for a moment listening to his wife's music. He kept trying to like it, to learn its rhythms and repetitions. But it wasn't Mozart and it wasn't Coltrane.

"Darling," he called.

The sound stopped and Grazia came into the bedroom and kissed him.

"For tomorrow," he said.

"It's gorgeous," she replied, looking at the pink and silver gown. "I'd already planned what to wear."

"I bought it at Trends."

"Expensive. Is it quite me?"

She held it up against her body and he stared.

"Everything is quite you," he said, amazed at his choice, his own excellent taste. He'd seen it in the window and known at once that it was right. The saleswoman had talked him into buying a silk pantsuit as well but he'd put that away for another time. There were half a dozen garments in her closet now, chosen by him, his eye for women's clothes a latent talent awakened by a youthful figure. "You'll look ravishing."

★★★

They'd argued early on about what she saw as his extravagance. The gold bracelet. The Mark2 watch. After all there was a planet out there to save. There were people everywhere in need. He explained to her that he could afford it. It helped the economy. Money made the world go round. His first wife, had she heard him, would have laughed in derision. When she left, she'd called him a tightwad but Jean wouldn't have looked good in the pink and silver gown and, in any case, their combined income then was a fraction of what he pulled in now.

★★★

The next evening when he was getting changed, Grazia said, "So tonight we're meeting the party fund-raisers."

"Not the fund-raisers, sweetheart, the donors."

"Right. The fat cats."

"We have to get to the club early."

"I'll be ready."

And, oh God, she was. A princess only lacking a tiara, she came down the stairs and whispered to him, "Why can't we stay at home and go to bed?" He thought about the Great Lakes Water Treaty to suppress desire, and led her to the car.

The event began at seven. She stood beside him, smiling and nodding, shaking hands, receiving people to whom much had been given and from whom much was now expected. Paul, standing there like his father outside church on those Sunday mornings long ago in Smiths Falls saying over and over to members of his flock, 'So good of you to come,' heard men murmur to his wife, "You're looking very lovely tonight."

"Thank you," she replied every time. It was in her to demur and say, oh this old thing, but she refrained and he was pleased. Beside her, the other women were drab, boring, old.

The herd moved on to graze at the buffet and lap up the free wine. Then Grazia mingled like a dream, smiling and listening, saying little. She was a natural in this charged political world, his world. He tried not to watch her, not to look possessive, not to be jealous of every man who came near her. At the same time, he was nervous that she might suddenly say the few words that could destroy a deal, upset a fragile arrangement.

Hank Allison, head of ABD and five-star bastard, came up to him and said, "I'd like a word."

Ten years ago, the guy wouldn't have given him the time of day. But now, in a tone that was all but deferential, he murmured, "We need to know how the Syrax bill is going."

"I can assure you," Paul said.

"We're grateful."

"I understand."

"Your wife is a great asset," Allison went on, nudging him and giving him a complicit grin. Paul grinned back. It was going to take some pressure on Dupuis and Williams to get their votes but he knew the magic words. By next week it would be sewn up.

He helped himself to a glass of champagne and sipped it. The expensive bubbles spelled success. He knew that they could also spell its opposite but dismissed that word and moved back into the fray. "Great that you could be here." "We've got JG on side." "I think I can guarantee a meeting with the PM."

★★★

On Monday morning, walking in the corridor, that corridor of power where he had never thought to walk, he bumped into bumptious Gregson.

"A success? Your little do on Saturday?"

"We got a lot of promises."

"Call them in, Paul. Pin 'em down. Don't let them eat bait and slip away. Keep after them."

"You bet," Paul replied.

"I'd like you to come to our cottage in the Gatineau next weekend. And bring Grazia with you. It'll be a small party. It's a pretty place, a bit of colour left on the trees."

★★★

"That's it. That is absolutely it," Grazia said, slamming her bag into the trunk on Sunday evening.

Paul didn't want to hear this. He turned and looked back at the so-called cottage, a six-bedroom palace on the edge of the lake. He'd enjoyed the weekend and would have liked to savour the memory of being out on the lake with three of the most important men in the country, chatting, laughing, talking football.

"All the guys wanted was to get me into a corner."

"But, darling."

"And those women. One more day in that so-called cottage and I would've pushed Ginny Gregson into the lake and held her down with a paddle."

"They can't help it."

"They can't help being middle-aged but they can help being snobby and looking at my clothes as if I'm a tart. I'm a threat. They worry that their husbands will dump them for someone young. And who could blame them? Sorry, women of the world, I didn't mean that."

"But, darling."

"Moreover, they don't talk about anything but politics. And I don't mean ideas, I mean who's getting what and taking what from whom. Who's up who's down. Who's worth talking to and who not."

He put his arm round her and told her she was right but it was part of the job. Six years ago, when he'd first seen her, Grazia was a junior delegate at the party convention and he was on the sidelines, observing. The graduate student gathering material for a paper on the shift in political demographics. She'd responded to his tentative approach with interest, enjoying their conversation. Because he could talk. He knew his history, he'd read biographies of the great political leaders. He'd wooed her with quotations from Disraeli and tales of early struggles in Upper Canada and jokes about Mackenzie King. They'd argued as friends and fought as lovers. And she was his, on his side, part of his team. He needed her.

Patiently he said, "One more, sweetie, please. On the twenty-fifth. At home. Just a few of the guys. Only a couple of hours. I think it will be a bit of a celebration."

"You want me to serve drinks and let them look down my cleavage!"

"And after that we'll go for a vacation. Europe. India. Anywhere you want."

"Spain," she said, turning her back on him, "I have a castle there."

"What?" he said and then smiled. She was kidding him again. But if everything went well in the next few years, maybe he would build her a castle in Spain. A small one. Near a beach. Footprints in the sand. Sunsets. Wine on the terrace. But not yet. Not yet.

He let her drive and got out his cell phone to tell Allison about the result of his weekend's work.

***

There was a light snowfall on the twenty-fifth. Paul was out early clearing the drive. When Grazia came back from her morning class, she told him there was no need to polish it and took the broom from him. Later he showed her the champagne that was to be served and then took her upstairs to their room.

"I thought you might wear this," he said.

He brought out the navy blue pantsuit and the caramel coloured shirt. With her dark hair and high colour, it would be perfect. She would be perfect.

"Perhaps," she replied and kissed him.

He took it as assent.

"I feel like one of those paper cut-out dolls that are only wearing panties and then you put different clothes on them. There are little tabs that hook over their shoulders."

"This is an important day for me."

"I know," she said.

"Finally some recognition for all I've done."

"You deserve everything you get, darling."

He went downstairs and left her to dress. Am I, he wondered but quickly dismissed the thought, treating her like a doll? He laughed to himself. She was a living, loving woman and who knew it better than he did.

The bell would ring in moments. The maid had stayed on for an extra hour to set out trays of hors d'oeuvres and to answer the door and show the guests in. Paul moved the arrangement of chrysanthemums and fall leaves to the desk and put it between the photograph of himself with the American Ambassador and the group picture in which he was standing beside the exotically dressed Finance Minister of Nigeria. He stopped for a moment to look at the picture of John at his high school graduation and let hurt and doubt creep into his mind. His only child despised him. And what the hell had he done to deserve that! He turned to the wedding photograph, second wedding, and put it behind the others. Grazia had chosen on that day to wear a two-piece in a white and pale green pattern that she'd bought secondhand. It scarcely fitted. Or as his mother said later, it fitted where it touched.

His mother resented losing a daughter-in-law she loved in spite of the fact that the woman had walked out on her son. At any rate she wasn't about to welcome a replacement with grace.

She still met Jean from time to time and he knew they talked about him and his 'trophy' wife and probably laughed. Well screw them all! Grazia loved him. And he loved her. When he saw her come into a room, he felt like kneeling down and praying. Though he wasn't sure to whom. He had accepted neither his father's God nor his father's narrow expectations.

Grazia's parents didn't come to the wedding. They saw him then as the destroyer of their daughter's bright future but came round when they smelled money. Screw them too!

The bell rang. The first guest had arrived.

It was Gregson looking more portentous than usual.

"Where's your lovely wife?"

"It takes her a while to get ready."

"But worth it, eh Paul!"

Paul had never thought of himself as a smirker but he knew that the look on his face was nothing less than a smirk. He rearranged his mouth.

Gregson said, "I'm early because I want a word."

Paul led the small man towards the fireplace and leaned against the mantel to steady himself. This was his moment.

Gregson said, "You came through, Paul. And we're grateful. The Party is grateful."

It was enough. They shook hands. The doorbell rang again and again. Twenty minutes later there were seven men in the room and no sign of Grazia. Paul had to suppress his good news till the announcement was made. He spun conversation out of air.

"Snow didn't stick around long."

"Ice on the canal soon."

"Somebody has to talk to the committee."

"You watch the game, Saturday?"

His 'lovely wife' was taking her time. But here she was. She made an entrance wearing jeans and an old wrinkled sweater that was too tight for her.

"You haven't served the drinks, Paul. What are you thinking?" She turned to the men and said, "He's very absent-minded these days. I don't know why. Not getting enough sleep maybe." She winked at them and went on, "Champagne, everybody? You all like that?"

She went out without waiting for an answer. The guests, waiting for a glass of wine, a glass of anything, were not comfortable.

She came back and said, "Which one of you handsome gentlemen will come and give me a hand?"

Gregson hurried to join her. Paul couldn't leave his visitors. More minutes went by before she returned carrying a tray with tumblers on it. Gregson followed carrying two bottles of champagne.

Paul looked at the labels and muttered to Grazia, "Not this. The other. Not those glasses."

It was too late. Gregson had popped one cork. Busch was loosening another.

"I didn't mean," Paul said, but couldn't bring himself to tell them that this was the cheap stuff he kept to mix with orange juice when he invited his staff to Sunday brunch. He tasted it. It wasn't even fucking chilled. He could smell doubt in the room. And there was Grazia waltzing round in those dreadful clothes pouring out twelve-dollar-a-bottle sparkling wine with Gregson glued to her side like a Siamese twin.

This was meant to be his moment, his hour, and she was behaving like the tart the other women thought she was, giving these men something to tell their wives when they got home. This is how they saw her. This was their image of his beloved. And she was fulfilling their expectations.

He said, "My wife has stupidly brought the wrong bottles from the kitchen.

"Let's have some of the real stuff, darling. And while you're out there, go and change.

"She's been jogging."

"No, I haven't," she said. "Not vertically and not horizontally either."

He went up to her and muttered, "Stop doing this, you stupid little bitch."

She threw the contents of her glass into his face. He grabbed her arm and slapped her.

She didn't scream or cry out but simply pushed him so that he flopped onto an armchair like a seal. She kept on smiling and offering more 'champagne' to his guests; guests who disappeared one by one as if they'd been made to vanish into thin air by magic.

He looked round the room but they were gone, every one, every single goddam one. Not one man had stayed behind to reassure him that it was all right: they knew he was not an abusive husband. He didn't go around hitting women. She was young, a bit crazy. They would forgive the warm, cheap champagne.

The platters of quails' eggs and caviar were untouched.

★★★

The setting sun was casting shadows on the bare branches of the trees in the garden.

In the middle of the lawn, his lovely wife was lighting a fire, something forbidden by the city. Then he saw that she was throwing onto the pyre thousands of dollars worth of outfits, everything he'd ever bought her. The clothes were giving off sparks like a bunch of firecrackers. The damp grass was beginning to catch fire. A little line of flame was creeping towards the hedge. He rushed outside for the hose. She'd got to it first and was calmly watering the ashes and the burnt lawn as if it were summer. He stamped on the random sparks and broke off a glowing branch of cedar. A jet of water hit his legs.

***

When it was safe, when there were no more orange patches anywhere, he took off his shoes and went to sit in the living room. He ate a quail's egg. Grazia brought him a mug of tea.

"So it's over," he said.

"It depends," she answered.

"On what?" he asked, grabbing at the straw.

"Come on, Paul. Is this the life you really want? Sucking up to people every day? Weaselling around. Making deals you don't even believe in."

"It took me a long time to get to this place. And you've ruined it. As if it was nothing. And now I'm nothing."

He couldn't look at her. He could only count the people in the family who'd let him down. Four not including his father: Jean had walked out of the marriage. His mother liked his ex-wife best. His son despised what he did for a living. And now Grazia had torn down the remaining structure of his life.

She was still talking, he listened to the words. "You gave me the impression that you had ideals. That you wanted seriously to affect policy. And you've turned into a lobbyist."

"I'm good at it. We do have an effect. It's important. It's what I do. What I did." He had used the past tense and saw himself, an actor in an old movie reeled backwards, walking away from everything that had made his life recently good. "And what am I supposed to do now?"

"Try to understand what you were doing to me."

"I was. You were. I mean." He looked at her, trying to figure out what he'd done that was so wrong. She was staring at him as if she wanted to draw blood out of him. He shook his head because he didn't know what to say or do to make things right.

And then Grazia said, "Are you really too old to learn new tricks, Paul?"

II

There were twenty-five young people ranged in a circle close to the small stage. The magician was in full rig, the black tailcoat and top hat, even the wand. How could there be magic without a wand to tap into its mysteries? The magician bowed. The audience applauded without enthusiasm and then sat back, bored and sceptical.

"The rings, please!" The Amazing Sandro demanded.

Jack, the blue satin pants rubbing against his thighs, and hating the tight silver top he had to wear, smiled the necessary smile and handed over the rope.

"My assistant is confused this evening," the magician said, feigning anger.

And then moments later, made the limp piece of rope form an apparently rigid line. Slowly and with apparent effort, she brought the two ends of the rope together to form a circle.

How did she do that? Easy when you know how.

Jack handed her the metal rings, holding up each one to demonstrate that it was complete, no breaks. Rapidly, she put them together, separated them. It was impossible. It was magic. The kids were not impressed. Had to be a catch.

She picked a stooge from the audience, a teenage boy who slouched forward, grinning at his friends as though he knew all the answers. She put three coins into his hand and made him close his fist. When he opened it, there were four, then two. The boy lost his assurance and watched closely but she was too quick for him. There was a flicker of interest.

The tricks were simple really. A matter of smoke and mirrors. Persuading people to look over there while you were doing something over here.

The coins took a while and Jack had time to look at the kids, boys and girls with sad surly faces, from a group home. They were against her, against everything. But she was good. She almost had them. It never took her long to weave a spell.

★★★

One of these days he would stand behind her and point to the hand she didn't want her audience to see. But then he didn't plan to keep doing this till 'one of these days' came along. If he hadn't needed the money, he would never have answered the ad in the first place. He just hoped and prayed every day that no one he knew ever saw him in this dumb outfit.

"Cards," Sandro hissed.

He handed them to her and she made half of the red pack turn blue.

"I can do that," one of the kids said.

"What's your name?"

"Rick."

"Come over here and pick a card, Rick."

He carefully chose what he thought must be the wrong one, the one that would confuse the magician. He pushed the card into the pack. A few passes and she pulled out the right one. He demanded to see the pack. It must be all queens of hearts. She showed him the normal set: four suits, every card different.

"Huh," was all the kid said.

Whose idea was it to entertain these delinquents anyway? They should have been outside kicking a football, kicking goal-posts, kicking at the adults who'd sent them here.

They were sniggering at Jack in his blue outfit and he could guess the names they were muttering to each other.

Their keeper came in and thanked Sandro and conjured up slight applause. The kids shuffled out as though released from chemistry class. That could've been me, Jack thought, if I hadn't had parents, if I'd gone in for stealing or bashing heads.

"Your place or mine?" Barbara asked on the way back to town. "I need a drink. There was hostility there."

"Your place," Jack replied. He couldn't see taking her home and introducing her to his Dad, her in that get-up and him in his satin pants and having to explain the job to him. "It diverted them for an hour anyway. Not happy kids."

Her place was a three-room apartment with a view of the canal. The shelves were stacked with books. More books were piled on the floor and magazines covered small tables. An exotic kind of smell clung to the shabby furniture. Ropes and scarves and fake flowers lay around in corners. And masks. Masks from Africa, from the West Coast, from Italy; some of them creepy. The large desk in the corner with its neat stacks of files and papers was where she did her real work, a different kind of juggling.

She changed out of her suit and put on a white gown with a cabbalistic design.

"I slipped up on the double card," she said. "Almost didn't get it out of the pack in time."

She began to throw a loop of rope into the air, trying to make it land over his beer bottle.

"I'm going to try the new scarf thing on Monday. If it doesn't work I'll make it into a joke. What I need, Jack, is for you to look sexier than ever. Do an Elvis. Push it out a bit. I'm not suggesting thrust. Just you know. And while they're staring at your equipment, I'll do the switch." She picked up a pack of cards and ran them from one hand to another as if she was pouring liquid between jugs.

"You'll be wanting me to strip next."

"It's a women's group. Might be a thought."

"And let them tuck money in my pants!"

"Fifty-fifty."

"Dream on," he said.

She picked up her wand and tapped him with it. "Disappear," she commanded.

★★★

He lurked on the street for a while and watched till the older man arrived and went into her building. He wondered if The Amazing Sandro performed her rope trick for him.

At the club that evening, the same older guy came in but didn't notice Jack in his bartender's role. He asked for a Scotch, single malt neat. A connoisseur or a phony? Hard to tell which. Nice suit. Possibly rich. Did Barbara sleep with him? He'd come to watch the show a couple of times but she had never introduced them to each other. Between serving drinks, Jack got out his notebook and jotted down the lines he overheard and descriptions of the people. Grist for his mill. If a guy in a ski mask would only come through the door and shoot the place up, he'd be a first-class witness. The police would find him reliable, observant. *And what do you do, sir? I'm the Magician's Beautiful Assistant.*

★★★

On Sunday morning, his mother was watching for him out the window. She was looking her elegant best and had brushed her hair back, no longer trying to hide the lines on her face. She was good with make-up.

He could smell beef roasting. There would be Yorkshire pudding. He would put on five pounds in an hour and the satin pants would be tighter than ever.

"There was a picture of your father in the paper," she said leading him to the kitchen. "He doesn't look happy. When I think."

He wished she wouldn't think. Not about that. It had been ten years, or was it twelve already. And five years ago, when his

Dad had remarried, she'd stirred up the resentment of the divorce and just kept on picking the scabs off old sores. He offered to stir the gravy. She slid the roasting pan out of the oven and there it was, the slab of meat with all the vegetables greasily nestled around it.

"How's your work?" she asked.

He'd forgotten to invent the usual tales on his way here so he said, "Nothing much new."

"Your father could get you a job as an intern. All those MPs he knows now."

"I like what I do," he said. "I like the guys I work with."

"But is there any future in it?"

Only if I become incredibly dextrous.

She brought out an apple pie. He asked for a very small piece.

"Mom," he said.

She was all attention at once as if he were still ten years old and about to tell her he couldn't go to school because he had a stomach ache.

"In fact, I'm working for a lawyer."

"That's wonderful. You'll go back to school and."

"She's mainly pro bono. Has another job on the side."

"I never heard of a lawyer having a job on the side. What does she do?"

He couldn't, could not, bring himself to tell because that would reveal his part in it so he said, "She gives talks to people."

"A speaker. She must be clever. Stick with her. How old is she? Is she nice-looking?"

My son is married to a lawyer.

He left her to her fantasy and went to tidy the kitchen and put the garbage out, wondering how soon he could leave and get back to the piece he was writing on the politics of style.

He made coffee and took the mugs into the living room.

His mother was sitting in her Madonna pose as if she'd dined on a light salad and a glass of water and was floating above the chair.

"I've taken up music again," she said. "My teacher is a fantastic man. He says I could have."

His mother had stopped finishing her sentences a long time ago.

"At any rate, I can retire next year and then I can devote more time."

He looked round the tiny apartment. Hardly room for a piano. She could have afforded more space but this was the home she moved to after she left him and his Dad and she remained in it as a reproach. To herself or to them? Nervous breakdown, she'd said at the time but it was something else, something he could now almost begin to understand.

He wanted to walk away himself, to go to university on the West Coast. But working at two jobs and selling articles at three cents a word to a free weekly journal wasn't going to get him out there any time soon.

As if she could read his thoughts, his mother said, "You haven't asked."

There was no way he was going to ask again after the last time. Dad's scathing remarks about writing stuff for idiots and his reply that it was better than pandering had led to a major rift. If Barbara were a real magician instead of a two-bit conjurer, she would be able to turn straw into gold. How big was the step from magic to miracle? Both required great faith, alas.

***

"This is a neat event," she said as they were driving to the venue next evening. "If they like us, they'll tell their friends and they'll tell their friends. And these people have friends, let me tell you."

"You'll have to get someone else soon," he said. "I'm getting more pieces in the magazine."

"And they pay what!"

"My Dad has money."

"And you're not speaking to him."

She was nearly old enough to be his mother but he wasn't going to let her tell him what to do. One night, after a long show in Kanata, they'd drunk a good deal of beer and he'd almost – almost – made a move on her. He could tell she wanted him but he'd got up and left while he could. Never sure now whether he should or shouldn't have but glad that he hadn't. She was attractive in a heavy kind of way, round body, great tits. But again, she was thirty-six to his twenty.

★★★

The women's book club had decided that an hour of magic would be their treat – a few tricks for Halloween. It was a grand house. The living room had to be twenty feet long and nearly as wide. The pictures on the wall, the candleholders, the little figurines were expensive and looked genuine. If Barb could conjure some of this into their box, it would be worth a few bucks. The women, various ages, various sizes, various outfits, all kinds of chic, were drinking wine and eager to be drawn into the mystery. One in particular, a young one, somebody's daughter maybe, stood up and introduced them: The Amazing Sandro and her lovely assistant. He bowed and they laughed. They laughed as though they'd already had a good bit to drink.

Barbara, serious in her tailcoat and black hat, began her spiel. She had a different line from other conjurors. She made it sound poetic as though if they only believed, only watched, their lives would be changed; she could take them to another sphere. *Follow me, people.*

She'd brought tricks suitable for the occasion. First she asked Jack to go round the audience and borrow a scarf, a watch, a ring. The woman who offered the ring held onto his hand and asked him to make sure she gave it back to him. There was a little low laughter. Barb tucked a small handkerchief into the hollow of her left hand and in the next moment pulled out a never-ending string of black and orange streamers.

How does she do it?

The watch was put into a blender and made into a milky liquid which Jack drank slowly, pretending to choke as he spat out bits of metal. A flower was pulled out of the scarf, and another and another, and in one of the blooms was the watch. The applause got louder. Wine was being handed round again and Barb offered to turn it into water. The woman he'd taken the ring from was amazed to find it in her glass. And now the magician said, "Will someone please dim the lights. My assistant will give those of you in front a rope to hold. Hold onto it tightly."

One or two of them touched him as he walked by, patting his butt. He refrained from swinging his hand back and whapping them on the jaw.

They were dazzled as Barb made a pattern in the air with lights and spelled out the name of their hostess. Those holding the rope discovered a flower in their hands when Jack took the rope away.

And it was over.

The applause went on and much of it seemed to be directed at him.

Afterwards, a woman hung around them, watching as they packed up and folded the box of tricks, everything in its right place. Jack glanced at her wondering why she wasn't going into the dining room with the others to eat. She glanced back, stared in fact. He sensed that Barbara was looking at him too. It was a triangle. He was being offered a choice. He knew where the money was. Barbara gave him twenty-five dollars a performance. The woman, the stranger, and those who came after her would pay much more. He could be back at school in six months. Worn out. A husk. A man who had given pleasure to many. He smiled as he thought of the boasting he could do to Jerry and Andy. The envy on their faces. Simulated envy maybe. After that, a best-selling book entitled, *The life of a young goat*.

They weren't invited to stay and eat.

As she pulled up at Pizza Heaven, Barbara said, "You were a hit with that little crowd.

And we've got three gigs in November and December is crazy."

"Why do you do it?" he asked as if he didn't know.

It was a skill she had. Something she was good at. A talent not to be wasted. She loved to mystify people.

"In fact, Jack, I'm truly thinking of starting to do it full time. I have to work up a couple of original tricks. We need an agent, a few TV appearances and we'll have a show of our own."

He held on to the pizza box and when they got to her place, she invited him to come up in a way that suggested more than the shared meal. She was offering him an eternity of magic. His young life dribbled away in rings and ropes and cards and coloured scarves and sex with randy middle-aged women. He saw himself at forty in a much larger blue satin suit, handing the rings and the rope to an arthritic Sandro.

Before Barbara could snap her fingers and utter any magic words, he hopped out of the car and ran. He'd gone several blocks before he realised that he'd left his tracksuit in her car and was still holding the pizza. Sitting down on a low wall, he ate several slices. He hoped that the passers-by who waved at him took him for a party-goer or a member of the ballet. What he was, in fact, was a prodigal son about to go home and apologise to his father.

★★★

He opened the front door quietly so that he could run upstairs and change before he was seen. But there was a ghost in the living room, the shape of a head against a chair-back. The old man was sitting in the dark and didn't even say anything when he put the light on. There was a strong smell of ash and of despair. So the lovely Grazia had gone, taken the money and rushed off to find someone new and young. He felt sorry for his father and regretted calling him a pander.

"Dad," he said.

No answer.

"You OK?"

Still no reply. Not only was his father, the prominent lobbyist and party hack, speechless, his suit looked as though he'd slept in it. Had Grazia decamped with absolutely everything even his clothes?

"I'm fine," his Dad said, not sounding fine but turning round. "What the fuck are you wearing?"

"You're a what?" he asked after Jack's explanation.

Music was coming from the kitchen and a smell of simmering pasta sauce. Grazia was there singing along to some operatic love song.

"You're still here?" Jack said. "What've you done to him?"

"You know how butterflies change into caterpillars or the other way round. At any rate they morph. Your Dad's morphing. It'll hurt for a while but he'll be beautiful when he's got through it. You don't need to worry about him."

When he was leaving to meet his friends downtown, Jack patted his Dad on the shoulder and gave him a little kiss on the cheek and said, "Everything will be all right." He was not sure what *everything* was or whether it would be all right but in years past, in bad times, it was what the old man had said to him.

III

Jack had called to say he was coming over to say goodbye later. Barbara was sorry to lose the kid. But he really hadn't the soul for it. Didn't understand the thrill of surprising people, hearing them gasp with wonder at illusions that were as simple as one two three once you had the knack of distraction. *On the one hand and on the other.* If he'd been keen, she could have taught him a trick or two. Meanwhile, The Amazing Sandro had to find another assistant. But right now, Ms. Grant the lawyer was in charge and could expect no gasps of amazement in this role and certainly no standing ovation.

The case as usual came down to money v. poverty. Their first lawyer had backed out leaving a couple with, it seemed, no hope of ever getting out of a debt trap. They were waiting for her in the dreary corridor of the courthouse. Their eyes beseeched her. If they'd been the whimpering kind, they would have whimpered. But their problems had obviously given these two a kind of stoicism that was beyond reason. They should have been shouting out against fate, against the system, against the landlord who had driven them to this. Why weren't they kicking against the pricks! She'd read the file and it looked hopeless. But she was a magician. Confidence was all.

"We'll win," she said.

"We have to, Miss Grant." Sharon Hagel was a small woman with red hair nicely cut. Her heavy winter jacket was too big for her as if she'd shrunk within it. Her husband Mike was wearing a well-pressed dark suit and carrying his coat.

She would have liked to set them on a magic carpet and fly them to a warm place, an island where soft music played and kindly people brought bring them food and drink.

"We will," she assured them, and realised that she had just

imagined them in a kind of heaven. For all their struggles these two weren't ready to die.

Mike had been standing back and now he came forward and spoke.

"It's like a lot of spoiled kids are playing with us like toys, tossing us around, one to the other, for their own amusement."

Obviously as a child he'd read tales from the old myths: stories of heroes whose fortunes were dictated by irresponsible gods.

"It's another day off work," Sharon said practically.

"It's not so much that. We're told, be here on such and such a day. She loses a day's earnings and I miss another interview and what's it to them?"

Neither of them was a candidate for the only job Barbara had to offer and neither of them was going to be impressive in court. It would take some fancy footwork to win this one.

An official came to announce that there was a delay due to illness: Come back on Tuesday at ten o'clock.

"You see," Mike said. "Our time isn't worth spit."

"Let's have coffee," Barbara suggested and took them to the cafeteria in the basement.

They should have been going over the facts but here was an audience and The Amazing Sandro couldn't help herself. She took sugar packets from the little bowl on the table and made them disappear and then found them in Sharon's hair, Mike's pocket.

Sharon smiled at her as if she were a clever child showing off. Mike looked at her with suspicion.

"You're a conjuror," he said.

"It's my hobby."

"And you can't do anything about stopping the bastard?"

She led them to talk about themselves.

Fifteen years ago Mike had been well on the way to being a hero himself. High School football had led to try-outs. A scholarship. An accident. Since then, a variety of jobs below his level. Sharon was taking computer classes at night and working in a deli during the day. When she was earning more, he planned to go back to school.

"Let's talk about your chances. Your ex-landlord is suing you for back rent and damages. You say – I know, I know, I believe you – the damage was not your fault but occurred because he failed to do repairs. And you gave fair notice. So why is he doing this? Why does he persist? That's what we need to know."

"Because he can't stand to lose. Because he's vengeful. Because . . . " Sharon said and stopped.

Mike shouted, "Because when she went to see him in his office, he made a move on her and she kneed him in the balls."

People turned. Three women at a nearby table applauded.

Without admitting her conflict of interest, Barbara said she would see them next week wishing, wishing that she could sort out their lives and wishing she'd never met the man who was giving them all this grief.

★★★

Plush chairs. A good rug on the floor. Expensive wood. Fresh flowers. So this was where he worked. The receptionist asked for her name.

"Sandro," she said. "Just tell him Sandro is here."

Larry Brown was the name he went by. She wouldn't have been surprised if he'd had others. He came out of his room, grinned when he saw her and went to embrace her. She pushed him back and he led her into his office.

"Why are you doing this?" she demanded.

"What exactly?"

"Persecuting two desperate people."

She mentioned their names. He shrugged.

"I shouldn't be talking to you," she said. "It's against all the rules but you're someone I know. Is it only money with you? Is that all it is, ever?"

"I have a business to run. I'm not hounding those people. It's my manager. Look, they don't pay the rent. They don't tell me when water's leaking from the toilet. The heating is off and the pipes freeze and they try to fix it themselves. Where have they lived before this? Under a bridge?"

"They are afraid. You and your satraps have made them afraid."

"Satraps! Nice word, Sandro. When do you have another show on? I love watching you make things disappear."

"I never asked exactly what you did. I had my suspicions."

"And now you know. I grind the faces of the poor whatever that means. I drive widows and orphans out into the snow every Christmas Day. Or I would but there's a law against it so I have to wait till January."

"Please, just drop the whole case."

"Oh right! And have all the indigents in the city move into my buildings and wreck'em. Thanks for the advice."

"Then I hope – I hope – that one day you'll feel afraid and desperate. And don't come round to my place for a drink any more, OK."

"You'll get over it. See you Saturday at the Willards."

She looked at the papers on his desk, some of them no doubt about the case, and wished she knew how to effect spontaneous combustion. Then she looked at him. He was tall, sharp-featured, beaky. It was his sense of power that had attracted her and she wasn't proud of the fact. Fortunately, their relationship was still spelled with a small r and was about to end with a large D.

She went out without saying anything. He called after her, "I'll tell the judge you were here," and laughed.

★★★

Jack brought her his uniform, the blue satin pants and sequined top, and told her again that he was through.

"Keep it," she said. "You never know. If my next assistant's a woman it won't fit anyway."

"No," he said, putting the package down as if it carried an infection.

She laughed and said, "Once a Beautiful Assistant, always a Beautiful Assistant. And by the way, there's one little thing you might do for me."

He was wary as if he imagined she could turn him back into a frog.

"All I want you to do," she said, "is pretend you're a thief."

"And if I get caught by a pretend cop?"

"Just a matter of a few papers."

"No."

"Well good luck, Jack."

"I'm off to UBC. My Dad's paying my fees. I'm worried about him. He's beginning to look happy the way people do when they go totally out of their minds."

"Aha," Barbara said. "Someone's cast a spell on him. Was there a smell of smoke or sulphur?"

"Smoke. Hey! You make everything into a trick."

"You were a great assistant."

"Thanks. I'll put it on my résumé."

He kissed her on the cheek and said, "I had a good time, really, Barb. You'll find someone else."

"I'll watch for you on TV and in the papers," she said. Unlike her, he would stick to his chosen career and become good at it.

Her parents had been thrilled when she told them she wanted to study law. They'd helped with the fees and encouraged her through the long dusty years. But it was the magic set they'd given her to keep her quiet on that long trip through the Rockies when she was ten that had started her on the road to mystification. Could she now sue her parents because her life was divided into two uneven parts and she wasn't sure which path to take? If she were truly interested in her career, she would put her tricks back in the box and concentrate on Law. Or she could sell the books and become a full-time enchanter.

She spent hours looking over the Hagel files, reading up on similar cases. There had to be something. Had to be! And there were only three days to go. If she argued that Larry had a history of harassing tenants, his lawyer would claim that Mr. Brown was a philanthropist who rented apartments to low-income earners and suffered great loss thereby: he was a good man who had no choice but, now and then, to make an example of bad tenants. There was photographic evidence of the damage done when Mike had tried to thaw the frozen pipes with a hair dryer.

★★★

The theme of the Willards' party was the supernatural – a wide range. Two hours to go and she had no costume planned. If she wore her Sandro outfit, they'd expect a performance. There would be several ghosts and aliens and it was much too late to find something original. She bent a wire coat hanger to make a halo but couldn't fix it onto her head. In the end, for want of anything better, she made a scythe out of a broom handle and a piece of stiff board covered with foil, put on her black robe and took with her the white mask she'd bought in Venice. She had to park two streets away from the house so she locked up the car, put on the mask and took hold of the scythe and the wine she'd brought along, and began to walk quickly. It was cold, beginning to snow, and she didn't want the scythe to come apart. A man in front of her turned back and saw her and then began to walk faster as if she were pursuing him.

"It's all right," she called out.

But he only hurried on and then stopped and leaned against a wall.

It was a trick. He would wait for her and then attack her. She surely didn't look like a woman in this outfit but she walked like one and that was enough for some of those guys.

She slowed down. To get to the Willards, she had to pass him. She put the scythe in the hand nearest the wall so that she could hit him with it if he made a move. But he turned his back to her and appeared to be breathing heavily.

She waved the scythe at him and said, "I know all about you," and walked on.

★★★

Larry was dressed as Julius Caesar, handsome in his toga and laurel crown. He said he'd misread the message and thought it was about supermen.

"Or, if you want, 'superpersons'," he said to Barbara. "You look grotesque."

"That's what it's about," she answered. "'Beware the Ides of March.'"

"It's October."

"It's a concept."

She kept away from him and danced with a Martian and then with a man wearing shorts and a T-shirt who said he was a 'heavenly body'. All the while she pictured the Hagels sitting in their apartment, worried about the case and wondering if their lives could get any worse. She should go home and make notes, more notes, think her way through till she found an answer instead of drinking wine and prancing around like an idiot.

Tina Willard turned the music down and shouted that it was time to present the prizes.

The first prize went to a werewolf. And then Tina said, "And the second prize goes to our favourite conjuror."

"We want a trick," someone called out.

"A trick!" Tina repeated.

Here it was. Time to sing for her supper. But there were thirty or so people in the room, all of them friendly, how could she resist?

"I haven't got my wand with me or my case," she said.

The assorted characters in the room were looking at her, demanding not to be disappointed. She was a magician. She could produce things from thin air.

"Give me a few minutes," she begged.

She asked Tina for some blank sheets of paper and wrote a few words on the top one.

"I need an assistant." She pointed her scythe at Larry. Reluctantly he came forward.

"The magic," she said, "will only work if it's performed by the pure in heart."

There was low laughter from the guests.

Larry was standing beside her murmuring, "Get on with it."

"This is a lawyers' trick," she said. "On this paper, I've written a few prophetic words about a case that might appear in court very soon."

She put the paper into the pocket of her gown.

"A scarf, please."

She was given a silky blue shawl which she folded and tied round Larry's face. She turned him round three times and tapped him on the head with the blade of her scythe.

"In and out and roundabout," she intoned. "Elves and goblins are abroad. If you've been evil they'll find out." When it comes to magic, everyone is a child.

She took the scarf away, pulled the paper from her pocket and waved it in front of Larry's face.

He read the words and angrily tore the paper into strips as she had hoped. She waved her scythe over the pieces and they became a whole sheet.

"Let's read the charges."

Larry grabbed the paper and shredded it again. The audience was delighted. Barbara made paper whole. They went through it one more time with Larry getting angrier and the guests seeing it as a prepared act.

Finally she picked a flower from Tina's hair and money from a monster's ear, and bowed to cheers and laughter and demands for an encore. She shook her head. She'd done what she wanted to do.

When the music began again Larry asked her to dance.

"All right!" he said.

"You're dancing with death."

"I hardly touched that woman."

"Which one?" she asked.

***

On Monday morning she got up early. She had to be prepared because there was no telling which way the cat would jump. She walked about practising her speech, trying to strike the right tone. The sound of the buzzer startled her.

"Who is it?" she asked through the microphone on the wall.

It was them, her clients. What was she to tell them? That she was useless and they would lose and become a totally bankrupt, homeless couple? Would she then feel obliged to give them shelter and food for the rest of all their three lives? You'll never be a great lawyer, Professor Harding had told her in her last year at law school. A decent one, maybe. She'd gone away determined to prove him wrong. But she was only a mediocre lawyer – and a fairly good conjuror.

And why had the Hagels come to her apartment? She must have given them the wrong card.

She invited them to come up and unlocked the door to let them in.

They entered laughing. Larry Brown had instructed his lawyers to withdraw the case. Had she not heard?

"Are you sure?" she asked. "I haven't been informed."

She fetched her cell phone from the bedroom and listened to the messages. There it was. Game over. Charges dropped.

Sharon kissed her. Mike felt in his pocket and brought out a small box wrapped in shiny paper.

"For you," he said. "We don't know what you did but it worked."

She tore off the wrapping and there inside the old velvet box was a brooch shaped like an angel.

"It's beautiful."

"From the old country," Sharon said. "His grandmother brought it with her."

"You truly are a magician," Mike said.

Barbara looked at the two of them. The relief in their faces was lovely to behold and somehow much more gratifying than applause. "Good luck," she said, as she showed them out. They would need it in their struggles against the world – and the mythic gods.

Time went slack. She had a free day. She had choice. It was cold but the sun was shining. She went for a walk along the canal and ended up at the office. There were papers to read, new cases, more messed up lives. She left at lunchtime and went to the Art Gallery to find perspective.

***

Larry called the following week and asked to see her. One last time won't hurt, she thought. She would not gloat. She'd made a guess backed up by slight verbal evidence and it had paid off. That was all. He came up to her apartment, not looking pleased.

"You've tidied up," he said.

"Thanks."

"My lawyer was furious about the Hagels."

"Good."

"I suppose you think you're clever. You and your lawyers' trick! It was taking advantage."

"That's rich."

"Are you going to take it up full time?"

"Being clever?"

"Stop fencing with me. You know what I mean?"

"There's more than one kind of sorcery. It's hard though to get a really good assistant. But you were great. Thank you."

The Shape of a Man

THEIR LITTLE BACKYARD was undecided. Was it still Winter? The tepid sun of the last few days had encouraged a few green shoots to emerge. He'd gone outside so that he could speak the words aloud softly to get the sense of them and maybe find that elusive last line.

"I am a thinking machine
Wired for sound
In a shape
In the shape of.
I walk the round world."

(He'd changed that from *walk round the world* because it seemed more poetic.)

"I'm a man
In a shape
In the shape of . . . "

And there it ended. He was stuck. Through the open door he could hear Jess shouting, "Shut! Shut! Shut up!!!" as if she was trying to stop him from thinking but she was only trying to drown out the voice of the leader of the free world. Her rage at the man had moved into a kind of madness. When she heard him on the radio saying words like *freedom* she would yell, "You are killing it." As for *democracy* . . .

He moved further away from the house.

In the shape of? There was no single short word for a sack

with a long thin projection from each corner and a large ball on top, except he supposed *human, or ape-like. Body* wasn't precise enough because there are bodies of water and bodies of work and anti-bodies and there was Alicia Body who certainly had an A-one shape not at all easy to define except with words like *luscious.* Ms. A. Body was part of his brief wild-oat-sex-lust life which now seemed as far off as Mars. Distant. Past. Good while it lasted. And where was Ms. Body now?

Jess called out to him, "Are we going to work this morning or not?"

The muse would have to wait. He put his notebook into his pocket and went to start the Hyundai.

He had to have a whole poem to read out to the class that evening. A new distinct eight-line verse. Something personal and original, Sue had said. Forget form for now. Give it feeling. But he felt that he had to explain his outline, his physical self, before he could move on to love or helplessness or anger or bitterness or deep sorrow or any of the emotions that the great poets were wont to express. He liked that last phrase. *Were wont to express.* It came from reading Tennyson and Wordsworth which Sue had told them not to do. Go for the moderns, she said, and had given them a list of fine Canadian poets some of whom were alive and well in this very city.

Jess strode out of the house, got into the car, and slammed the door.

"Why do you listen to the news in the morning?" he asked.

"If I didn't turn it on, I'd know he was in there mouthing off anyway," she said. "And that would be worse because I wouldn't know what he was saying."

"I think we both need a vacation," he said.

"Dreamer," she replied.

He dropped her off at Androids to Go to spend her day designing futuristic home helpers in the shape of Robots. ATG's squat square vacuum cleaner, known as SQV and programmed to scuttle about the floor and get into corners and under furniture, was a hot item for busy people. It could be timed to work while they were out. Only one of the little machines so far had given the family pet a fatal heart attack. The SQV that had chewed up a valuable rug had been, so the company insisted, miscued by its owner. ATG had, though, paid compensation for the cat, and agreed that some adjustments were needed. The company was still looking for the optimum shape for the little robot and were considering round.

By the time he got to his own office it was nearly 8.30 and there was panic in the air: the proposal for the new communication system had gone to Kuala Lumpur instead of Kabul. Whose fault was it? They were wasting time looking for a culprit instead of sending a copy to the right place. Alec in his corner was making dumb remarks as usual: Why not Kandahar or Kensington or Kelowna? Saner voices were saying, We need a messenger. We need someone on the ground. We have to rectify this error. Someone must go over there and pretend that we planned to hand deliver it in the first place. How could they get contracts if they were seen to be inefficient? The cost of a plane ticket was peanuts in relation to the possible rewards.

He knew he was being fingered and kept quiet because he wanted to go and apparent eagerness could ruin a chance like this. When Cheryl called him into her office, he waited until she told him to arrange the trip and then simply nodded acceptance as though it was a burden he would bear bravely for the sake of the company.

"You'll need warm clothes," she said.

The others made jokes about a Kevlar vest and asked if he knew how to fire a Kalashnikov and pretended to shoot at him.

"I am only packing good will," he said, "and a confident smile."

***

That evening Jess said, "You're going where?"

"Afghanistan." He tried very hard to keep the excitement out of his voice.

"And we know who made a mess of that country, don't we."

"It took several governments to screw it up. Sequentially. Over a long time."

"But now. I'm talking now!"

For weeks he'd wanted to get away from her rage. Either that or find some way to calm her down. Her political sense was acute and she was often right, at least according to him and to the newspapers they both read. And he did care. But it was time for her to come down to the small and the local. In effect, to him. To pay attention. Tomorrow he was going to set off to a wild and alien land that was unsafe and volatile. He wanted to skip and kick his legs together in the air and shout, Yippee. But he also wanted Jess to be concerned for him. At least a little.

"Honey," he began.

"No," she said.

"What's for dinner?"

"Cuban chicken."

***

He always worried about the slow cooker. Was food that was left to bake on low heat all day ever quite safe or did the germs just copulate in there and multiply? His mother had cooked food hard and killed microbes, taste, vitamins all in one blast. She might as well have used a blowtorch. But all of her six kids had survived to adulthood without a single case of food poisoning between them. His Dad's chronic indigestion was put down to heredity.

He began to think about the poem again. It was what you ate that gave you your shape. In the shape of a burger . . . And in Afghanistan, the shape of a sheep's head. He'd lost the sense of it. He'd lost the sense of Jess too and here they were in the shared house, living together, eating together, exchanging words. What did it mean?

The street they lived on was a cul-de-sac. Ten years ago when they'd decided to move in together, they chose the small house because it was sturdy and the bedroom window framed a mountain view. And at night, downtown Vancouver was a jewelled stretch of dark velvet. Jess liked it because she knew it would be a quiet place. He liked it because it was the first house he'd ever owned. Even though he only owned half, it was his home. Driving towards it in the evening had given him deep pleasure until lately, until anger had moved in to make of their household a *ménage à trois*.

"The trouble is," Jess said, "that you are a pushover. Cheryl knew you wouldn't say no."

He looked out the window and could see the lights in both floors of the house opposite. Jason and Sandy were dividing up their belongings, about to separate, fighting over possession of the dog.

He began to assemble the salad, shaking the lettuce, cutting up celery, slicing walnuts.

"Glass of wine?"

He said yes please because he had an adventure ahead of him and felt guilty about it. Maybe it would be best to forget the poetry workshop and stay home. But the poem had been nagging at him all week. The fourth line with its neat four syllables was fine but he couldn't end the whole poem with a preposition. There was nothing wrong, Sue said, with concrete words. Poems needn't be all obscurity and flowers. He wanted to finish it with a knock-out word. He grasped at phrases. In the shape of a doll? Too easy. In the shape of a clown perhaps. In the shape of a question mark.

He went to the cupboard under the stairs and got out the smallest travel bag.

"So this is you going away," Jess said.

In the shape of a plane. In the shape of a bird.

"You'll fly to Europe. Or are there direct flights to Kabul from here?"

"To Frankfurt and then Moscow and so on."

"And so on?"

"Do you mind?"

"At work today we planned a sales strategy for SQV. I might take it to the Fair in New York except that I'd rather not go there. I told Gerry so but he laughed. It looks, I said, like a bomb. You won't be carrying it in your hand, he said. We'll send them on by courier. Purpose of your journey, they'll ask in customs. To demonstrate small electronic devices that can be programmed ahead of time. You can see what would happen."

He was laughing at her imagined scenario but then he saw that she was crying.

"You don't have to go, love."

"I will go."

She was crying, he knew, for injustice, for the wronged and the tortured, the exiled, the threatened and the fearful. There was nothing in all the chaotic world that he could sort out for her by himself. Even Hercules would have been helpless, overwhelmed. There were no useful words to put on her wounds.

He sat beside her and wiped her tears and reflected that she was kind, she was sensitive. She had never once made fun of him, teased him about going to poetry classes, never said to their friends in a mocking tone of voice, He's an engineer and he thinks he's a poet.

After a few moments, she went upstairs to wash her face.

He read over the words he was to say when he presented the proposal to the company bosses in Kabul. This will revolutionise the city. Over time, it will connect the centre of the country to its outer edges. For now, a sturdy, fairly foolproof, system with message boards and decent bandwidth and a reliable telephone system will bring the place into the twenty-first century. He'd leave those last words out. Mustn't sound patronising. The system wouldn't help the poor and the oppressed, yet. And maybe unfortunately it would help the poppy farmers sell their product and the warlords to extend their power base. But in time. In time . . .

Jess returned. She had taken off her office clothes and was wearing velvety pants and a sweater. He looked at the shape of her. Like him, she was an oblong sack with the same projections and head but with different bulges. He got out his notebook and wrote, In the shape of a heart. It hardly made sense and wasn't entirely true but he liked it. Sometimes the first thing that comes into your mind . . .

★★★

And then he understood that he hadn't really been looking at her. She was right to find the world unsafe when she listened to the news. Instead of walking away, he should have been talking to her. Talking and listening. Trying to make sense. Looking to a future. Maybe he could tell her that his trip to Asia was a tiny effort towards a better world and that they must eventually get back to laughter, to proportion and find some glimmer of light in the chaos or they were wasting life, helping no one.

"I'll read my poem to you," he said, "instead of going out tonight." He turned his back to her so that he wouldn't be able to see her reaction. And he began to read.

"I am a thinking machine
Wired for sound.
In the shape
In the shape of.

I walk the round world.
I'm a man
In the shape
In the shape of a fool."

Jess, spooning out the pieces of possibly poisonous chicken onto rice, turned to him and smiled. "Be very careful over there," she said. "I don't want to hear about you on the news in the morning."

The Arena

How could he not see? How could he not understand? It was obvious to a child of three that there was a disaster out there waiting to happen. He was an overweight, under-brained idiot in league with the enemy. In wartime, he could have been denounced and shot as a collaborator or at least had to parade, his head shaven, naked through the streets. Two days ago, she'd gone out in the kayak and brought back a bottle full of water and offered it to him to drink. He had laughed.

Gloria kicked the fridge till it rattled, and shouted, "And God knows what it's doing to the fish."

It was time for the meeting and she had to decide on power dressing or casual. She'd walked behind women her size who wore jeans and it wasn't usually a pretty sight. Nonetheless, she put on her best pair and a grey and blue shirt: a fighting outfit.

The room smelled of public responsibility. And they were there in force, the men and women of Gorse Bay. In suits, in jeans, in skirts, T-shirts, frilly blouses, ball caps, a hundred and twenty-three concerned citizens were waiting to hear from their elected representatives. Gloria knew how many there were because she counted the empty chairs as she came in. She said random hellos to those she knew, smiled at the ones who were on the right side, ignored those in the wrong.

Five minutes later, the six council members walked onto the platform and sat down. They shrank back into their chairs behind the table as if they were expecting a fusillade of rotten tomatoes or worse. But to start with there was only a low undercurrent of complaint.

Marci Plastow in her role as chairperson stepped forward.

"I know why you're all here, " she said. "And we appreciate so many of you coming out on such a fine evening. I guess a lot of you would rather be on the water."

"Better on it than in it," somebody yelled.

"We have made our decision and we know that it won't be agreeable to all of you but we hope that."

"Get on with it." That was Ginny from the coffee shop.

"In a democracy," Marcia went on.

"Democracy!" a voice yelled. "You mean you've gone with the jocks."

"Shut up and sit down, tree-hugger."

"We've been betrayed."

Marci tried again, "After a great deal of discussion."

She was drowned out.

Gordon stood up and shouted, "Listen!"

He was bigger than Marci and louder and Gloria wished she'd brought half a brick to throw at him.

"As a matter of fact," he said, "speaking as your deputy chairperson, going with what we've heard from all of you and what we feel to be best for the town, we all know that there has to be a new sewage system. But maybe we're not ready for it."

"Not ready!"

"The beach is polluted. Our kids can't play there."

Marcia sat down and let Gordon take over and explain that fiscally they would be better off for the time being to spend the money on a new arena. The curling tournament might come their way in two years' time. It was important to have a show place and the competition would bring money to the town.

Half the people in the hall applauded.

The other councillors rested their hands on the table like children who'd been told to sit quietly. Two of them were unhappy. Jimmy Brydon scowled at Gordon then jumped down from the platform with a loud thud and stomped out of the hall followed by a third of the audience.

★★★

That night in the bedroom, Gloria watched Gordon take off his jacket and tie.

It would have been easy to choke and kill him but like all kinds of plaguy animals, there were many others where he came from.

"So," she said.

"I'll have more time at home now that's over."

"So you think it's over?"

He stood there looking at himself in the mirror, not displeased. She could have told him that there were pouches under his eyes and that his air of smugness was repellent but she only said, "You've changed."

"It's the best thing for the community."

"You mean it's the best thing for Marci Plastow's company. You've been bought."

He looked misunderstood. He was good at it.

She took the sheets off her bed and went to the spare room. Of course she couldn't get to sleep. The pro-arena group had spun a bogeyman out of development: along with a main sewage system, a 'big box' store would appear and an immense ugly mall. Berta would lose her bakery, Ginny's customers would desert her cosy place for Starbucks. Five-storey apartment blocks would go up overnight and be instantly occupied by a stream of undesirables from the city who were packed and ready to move at the first flush.

Gloria tossed and turned and tried to figure out a way to bring the council and half the people in town to their senses before it was too late.

She got up early and went out to the coffee shop. Let him make his own breakfast. The place was abuzz. She moved to the losers' side of the café where people were shaking their heads and making statements.

"This is a backward move."

"We're third-world."

They were also waiting a long time to get served. Ginny Denver wanted to try for a concession at the arena, stupidly ignoring the fact that she might well be out of business when the chains took over.

The triumphant were talking loudly about pristine forest, keeping their town small and lovely and the advantage of having a great place to skate. The shouting match began when Horst Bergman called over to Gloria, "You should listen to your old man."

"He's not my old man," she yelled back, disowning her husband of twenty-two years.

"You want your kids to swim in that water?"

"There's a pool."

"Wait till someone dies."

"You three over there can forget next Saturday."

That was Juli Svenson, speaking to former friends, rescinding invitations to her daughter's wedding.

Harriet Beale said, "That's not fair. We've bought outfits. And Jeannie made the cake."

"She knows what she can do with her cake."

The township wise woman, Imelda O'Connor, stood up and demanded quiet. She waited for the muttering to die down. Imelda had a wardrobe of long skirts and coloured jackets and hats that she wore according to the season. This day she was wearing a navy linen skirt and a pale green jacket. She was said to be eighty but her face, sun-baked from years in the bush, was that of an ancient crone. She glared round as at an unruly class.

"What kind of people are you?" she demanded. "You make the mess and you can't get together to clean it up. I have a question. How many of you here are on septic tanks? "

There were nods and grunts of admission. They waited for Imelda to say more but she simply sat down and bit into her cranberry orange muffin.

The uproar began again. What did that have to do with it? Imelda had obviously lost it. Whose side was she on?

"Septic tanks are fine as long as they don't overflow, and get properly cleaned."

"Main sewers are the only sanitary way to go in a town this size."

Jimmy Brydon took his coffee outside and leaned on the wall like a huge sulky boy. He'd been hoping to expand his trail-riding business but till there were main sewers he could do nothing. On her way out, Imelda spoke to him for a moment before she got onto her bicycle and pedalled off down the road.

On the way home, Gloria decided not to go to Berta's Bakery for her usual two loaves of whole wheat. It would be consorting with the enemy. Instead she bought a white loaf of no real sustenance at Horst's supermarket. As she walked towards the park, two of her neighbours crossed over to the other side of the road to avoid speaking to her. Even the Vergas' dog, usually a friend, turned its back when she walked by.

★★★

It was a silent Sunday. Gordon dug around in his raised vegetable beds. Gloria vacuumed the whole house and cleaned out the bedroom closet. She cooked a chicken for dinner with new potatoes and a salad, and sat in front of the TV with her plate on a tray. She could hear him clearing away in the kitchen and then going out.

Monday started out silent too. At the office, only necessary words were addressed to her. It was a hot day and her corner was a heat trap. She got on with typing up a proposal for the new parking lot beside the swimming pool till her keyboard was sticky with sweat, then she walked over to Bernie Travers' desk and took the only fan and plugged it in beside her so that she could feel the cooling breeze. As if she needed more chill. Bernie stared at her but said nothing. The boss came in late as usual and stopped in front of her to say, "This is a business. We have a chance to bid on the exterior of the arena."

On a piece of paper, Gloria calculated how far her savings would go if she quit, if she left Gordon, if she began a new life, if she moved to the city.

She gave herself the afternoon off and went home to do some baking.

★★★

Imelda lived in a cottage on the river. She cared little for plants. She wasn't one of those old women who grew herbs and lavender. Her yard was a mass of rocks and overgrown shrubs. She'd seen no reason to adapt to small town prettiness. Others could train clematis to climb up their fences and encourage fuschia; she had better ways to spend her time. No one knew exactly what those ways were but it was said she was writing her memoirs.

The old woman's reputation as arbiter had come about after the dispute over the new landfill site had caused one divorce and a street brawl. She'd told people to sit down together in the hotel bar and write out the pros and cons. After a long evening, a good deal of beer, some give and take, the matter was settled. She had also straightened out the matter of the town's attitude to Herb Wischen's return from jail and now when she spoke, people listened.

Sitting on a rickety wicker chair on the little porch, reading a newspaper, dressed in red, she was a tribal chief ready to receive supplicants. Two of her cats and her German Shepherd were lying around close to her. Animals she loved. Children she pitied. She had long ago divided the human race into two categories, fools and 'damfools,' and kids had no choice but to become one or the other. She kept a store of treats for the poor things and when the few who dared came to visit 'the witch,' she told them stories of ancient times when the world was a nobler place.

"See this," she said when she saw Gloria. "Price of gold. Up and down like a yo-yo."

"Oh," Gloria said.

"I don't know what to tell you," Imelda said.

"I haven't asked anything."

"That one of your cranberry nut loaves?"

"Yes."

"Set it in the kitchen, dear."

Gloria went inside the cottage. There was an array of casseroles and baked goods on the counter. She recognised Marci Plastow's orange cake. Jenny Croft's lasagne. A tuna casserole. A loaf of plain white bread – had to be Horst. Had Gordon also been by and brought the old woman a case of beer?

"You've had a bunch of visitors."

"Damn right."

"I guess they want to know what you think."

"Nastiness builds up like gas in a mine and then explodes."

"They should see that there's no time to waste."

There was a pause while Imelda went on reading her copy of *The Miner* and Gloria wondered if she could take the cranberry loaf home with her.

"What did you mean about septic tanks?"

"Live in shit, die in shit."

Half an hour later, after tea and orange cake, Gloria left with unpleasant images in her head and wished she hadn't come.

★★★

Gordon said, "We can't go on like this."

Gordon said, "Will you sleep with me?"

Gordon had not made dinner. His work was suffering, he said. I might lose my job, she responded.

In the morning there was a pile of manure on their doorstep so large there was no way to step round it and they had to use the back door.

"That's aimed at you," Gloria said to him. "You clear it up."

"It's you they're after."

"You're the one who wants to keep living in it."

The nasty pile was still there in the evening, a pleasure ground for assorted flies.

Determined not to give way, Gloria went out and had a hamburger at the Blue Moon. When she returned, the smell was still there but the pile was gone leaving only a stain on the front step. There was no sign of Gordon.

There was no sign of Gordon at nine o'clock. Or at half-past.

She walked down to the end of the yard. The manure was spread neatly over the raised beds and Gordon was lying face down on his cucumber plants. She screamed. And then with a great effort turned him over.

"I'll get help," she said, and ran to the kitchen to call 911.

She walked up and down the hospital corridor. Nurses came out of his room wearing masks. Juli and Bernie, setting aside the conflict, came to join her.

"It depends how long he'd been there," Gloria told the other two, tears in her eyes. "He must've been overcome by the smell or something."

Juli said, "And he was lying in it?"

"Lying in it," Bernie repeated. She stifled a laugh.

Juli began to shake. In a moment all three of them were giggling and couldn't stop. When the doctor came out to say Gordon would be all right but might have a little post-traumatic stress disorder, they had to pretend to be crying with relief.

★★★

There was laughter in the stores and the cafés for a day or two and then whispers and innuendoes ran about the town like ferrets. Some said Gloria had pushed Gordon into the muck. But mainly everybody wanted to know who'd left the potentially fatal pile on the Gribbons' doorstep. No witness had come forward. The house was a little way off the road and the deed had been done in darkness. It came down to motive, opportunity, and access to manure.

Sitting beside him on the couch, trying to tempt him with fresh strawberries, Gloria told Gordon he was lucky she'd come to look for him when she did. He grunted. He kept brushing his hand over his face and screwing up his lips as if he wanted to spit something out. He appeared to have lost interest in the garden.

On Thursday, Imelda came to see him. She swished up the path in her long cream skirt and walked by Gloria straight to the living room and said to Gordon, "How'd it taste, Mr. Gribbons?" She closed the door and stayed with him for twenty minutes. On her way out, she said no thank you to Gloria's offer of coffee and turned back to Gordon to say, "You see, you can have your cake and eat it."

That evening, Gordon ate a good dinner but said he was still feeling a little weak and asked Gloria if she would please drive him to the Plastows and make a detour via the stables on the way. He left her sitting in the car and went to the office on his own. After five minutes, he came out rubbing his fist and smiling. Jimmy Brydon followed him holding a hand to one side of his face but also smiling.

He said, "I'll start the ball rolling."

"We can do this," Gordon called back to him.

By morning, that phrase was the watchword in town. There would be fund-raising. Sponsorship. It would take more than a few bake sales to do it but there could be an arena as well as a main sewage system.

Why hadn't they thought of it themselves?

Imelda only smiled and said it was like prospecting: you could get fixated on one spot while just down river there was paydirt.

★★★

The tables were decked out in blue and white, and streamers and balloons hung from the walls of the Bay Hotel Grand Ballroom. Alone on the dance floor, Juli Svenson's daughter waltzed with her new husband round and round and round. Friends and family applauded and raised their glasses to honour the happy couple. Everyone who'd been invited was there. Later on, dancing with Gordon, Gloria thought to herself, He's a turkey at times. But at least he's a turkey who can be persuaded to change his mind.

Shades of Blue

ANDREA RANG THE BELL and knocked, and knocked again more loudly. When there was no answer, she tried the door and pushed it open. She could see at once that nothing was right. Even the cat appeared to be stunned into silence. John was sitting at the table staring ahead of him and didn't turn to greet her. Was it death? she wondered first. Or had the cloak of inspiration settled over him and given him the idea for a new mural? At any rate, there was nothing to do but say hello and hope the sky didn't fall in.

"Hello," she said.

"Ah."

He wasn't the age to be stricken by a stroke. Forty-three and healthy as a pig, he'd always seemed to be happy enough for a man who didn't have a regular sex life. She waited a moment. The room was untidier than usual. Magazines dripped from the tables to the floor, beer bottles were lying around near the fireplace, a painting shirt draped the back of the couch. But more significant than anything was the sight of him sitting still. These were his working hours and he was not working.

"You OK?"

"Mm."

"I'll get on then," she said, and went to the kitchen to cut up the onions and carrots she'd brought with her.

Her mother said the man was taking advantage and she'd replied that he hadn't yet and her mother told her not to be so sharp. It was a barter arrangement, perfectly fair: on Mondays and Wednesday evenings, he gave her painting lessons. On Saturdays, she cleaned the place and made a stew or a casserole he could eat for three days. He'd never yet asked her to pose nude for him. If he did, she was prepared to say no or yes depending how she felt at the time. This was one of the days when she would have answered yes and fallen nakedly into his arms.

Those two evenings were the bright moments in her week. She left behind the problems with her next essay, the strife at home, the hours she put in at the deli counter, and looked at the world through John's eyes. He showed her how to improve her brush strokes and told her to go to galleries further afield. Nothing prevented her from going to Vancouver or Seattle to spend a day looking at paintings except the time it took to go by ferry and the cost of staying overnight and her fear of standing too long in the presence of the great. The distance between her daubs and their creations was galactic. She would never get even part of the way towards their brilliance.

The kitchen looked different today too. The coffeepot felt cold. There were no dirty dishes in the sink. His private life was none of her business. She chopped the beef into cubes and added it to the vegetables. If some tragedy had struck, he would talk about it or not. Seasoning and stock went into the pot last. At least he had a decent collection of casseroles and copper pans. Perhaps if she put her hands on his shoulders and murmured soft words he would break down and put his head on her breast and tell her that he had terminal cancer and she would promise to look after him to the end. She reached for the jar of bay leaves.

His kitchen was a glory of colour. Mugs and plates in vivid reds and blues were ranged on open shelves. On the longest wall, he'd painted a scene of muted debauchery: modern satyrs and nymphs cavorted round the shelves of a supermarket stroking the cans and packages and each other as they danced in bare pursuit. He called it 'Bargain Hunting'. If her mother ever saw it she would tell her to come home at once, the man must be a pervert. *It's art, Mom.*

She put coffee into the filter and water into the tank and the plug into its socket.

There was still no sound from the other room. He and the cat were as quiet as mice. Perhaps he was stunned by desire. He was going to declare that he wanted her to live with him and be his only love. They would be married in spring. Her mother would shriek, You are only twenty, and her father would say, You're on your own now. After the honeymoon, she would teach John how to cook so she too could spend most of her time painting the figures and landscapes that her mother called 'bleak'.

John said she must always pursue her own vision, only improve her use of colour and her approach to design. I always want a picture I can climb into, he said. Maybe he had done just that, climbed into one of his own paintings and left his husk sitting in the chair. Or had the contract for the atrium in the new bank been cancelled after he had bought paint and spent six months sketching his version of early life in the province? She carried one mug of coffee to the living room and moved a pile of magazines and set it down on the glass table beside him.

He grabbed her arm. "You forgot milk."

She pulled away from him. "You don't take milk."

"Arachne does."

She decided to humour him and fetched a saucer of milk and set it down beside the cat which at least meowed a kind of thanks. Used to eating in the kitchen, the animal had to think Armageddon was at hand. And perhaps it was. John talked sometimes about the terrible state of the world. No country appeared to want to make peace. They preferred killing and wrecking to curing Aids in Africa. Starvation and poverty were riding roughshod over millions and only a few dedicated people seemed to care. Making bigger and more deadly weapons had become the aim of great nations. There was plenty of reason for him to sink into utter despair. And her too, but she had picked out a narrow path and wanted to give art a chance at least for a few years. After that, and if she failed, she would attend to the world.

"I'll do the cleaning."

"No need to go upstairs."

So that was it! He'd murdered the woman who now and then came from Calgary and stayed the night and her body was lying on the bed, a plastic bag over her head, blood dripping onto the hand-knotted rug from Iran.

Andrea sat down in the kitchen to drink her own coffee. She wanted to go home but home was not a refuge. This was her refuge and now the soul of it, the engine that made it hum, had run out of gas. It wasn't fair to expect him always to be the same or for her to feel as she did at the moment that he was letting her down. For seven months, she had come to this house three times a week to be greeted with a shout of, Andrea, come look at this. Or, Bring the coffee, Joan. He teased her because she hadn't known how to pronounce Miró's first name and thought he was a woman. *He was a Catalan, sweetie. From Catalonia.* The foreign words, the exotic images, the expanse of colour and ideas in this place had brought her far into that other world and now, it seemed, for today at least, the door to that world was closed. *This is self-pity*, she said to herself. *The man is unhappy. Tomorrow he'll be fine.*

She wasn't prepared to run the vacuum cleaner round his feet or to disturb the cat but, aside from the upper floor and the studio behind the house, there was nothing else to clean. She always left the kitchen till last, scrubbing the floor and backing out of the door so as not to walk over the wet tiles. She washed her mug and dried it slowly, thinking of words to say. The words he'd taught her to consider, *pigment, perspective, priority,* were no use in this particular case.

Her Dad would have told him to get off his ass and do something. But her father viewed the artistic temperament, not that he thought in those terms, as something self-indulgent and even perverse. People, especially men, were meant to get out there and labour even if that labour was not driving heavy machinery but sitting in an office and interviewing people who wanted a job. *There are people out there with a right to be depressed.* Those with money and a home and enough to eat were not in that class.

She looked through the living-room doorway. No change. Quietly, she went up the stairs. He hadn't said she mustn't go, only that she needn't. There was an ocean of difference. The stairs creaked but no yell came from below to tell her to come back down. She crossed the landing and stood in the bedroom doorway. The room was totally dark. Putting on the light would be a serious act. She thought of Bluebeard. She also thought of the book John had given her at Christmas so that she could learn about the infinite shades of blue. Stare at the *Portrait of Madame Matisse,* he told her, until you know what blue means. And she had stared at the doll-like face, the elegant orange scarf, until she'd forgotten all the names she'd ever known for blue: turquoise, aquamarine, sapphire, cobalt. Look at the dancing figures and see the joy in that movement, he said.

★★★

John had always treated her like a friend and now she was about to betray his trust. For his own good. How could she help him unless she knew the worst? She walked to the window on tiptoe and drew back the drapes. The bed as usual looked as though he'd wrestled with demons in the night. The pile of detective novels was neatly stacked on the bedside table, the lamp was upright. No pale hand reached out from under the bed signifying a corpse beneath. Nonetheless, she bent down to look. The only clues were a week's accumulation of dust and a single sock.

Then she straightened up.

The first thing she saw in the dresser mirror on the far side of the bed was her own face. Behind her own familiar features was a shocking backdrop of bloody violence. She closed her eyes and made herself turn round. *It's only paint. Only brush strokes and colour. Nothing to harm you unless, like Bluebeard, he comes and finds you.* She opened her eyes slowly, hoping the images had gone and that she would see only the usual bare wall.

The horror was still there. He'd washed over the green with white and divided the space into six vertical cartoon-like strips. Across the top was a frieze of skulls. In the first scene, a man wielding an axe was standing over a woman who was sitting with her back to him sewing the edge of a large sheet. In the next picture, the woman had turned and seen him and her face was frozen in a scream that was as much snarling rage as fear. Andrea recognized nothing in that face. The woman wasn't even young. The dress she was wearing covered her whole body from her neck to the floor. She wanted to turn away but had to follow the sequence as the woman raised her outsize pair of scissors to strike the man. Finally, they lay together on the ground, both bleeding, their faces, in odd contrast, gazing peacefully towards her.

She made her way quietly downstairs and sat in the kitchen and tried to stop shaking. It was the place where he slept for Chrissake! Could he ever close his eyes in that room again? Could she ever look at him again and let him guide her hand along the canvas, making the brush and paint obedient to her ideas, without thinking of all that blood and terror? And where was the man who had told her to look at Matisse, Monet, Renoir?

There were footsteps. The cat skittered by. John was standing behind her with his hands on her shoulders. She let out a dry scream.

"You were up there."

"Yes. I saw it."

"Didn't I tell you not to go? You know what happens to curious cats."

She couldn't speak or move. Her mother would weep for her. Her father would track John down to the ends of the earth and kill him. If she turned and grabbed him, he would throw her to the floor. He was twice as heavy as she was. She sent up a prayer to a God she hardly knew and kept very still.

After a moment that seemed like an hour, he sat down in the other chair and said, "I wasted all that paint and time. It took me two days. And now I've no way of getting it off the wall."

"You could, we could, paint over it. I'll help you. I'll go buy the paint," she said, stumbling over her words in relief. There was nothing now between her and the back door except three giant strides.

"Paint over it! You idiot. You little unknowing stupid bitch. It's one of the best things I've ever done. I woke up on Thursday night and began and didn't stop. I was inspired. I've never worked in such a rush before."

Andrea breathed again. She looked at his face. No cruel lines had been etched there since Wednesday. Fangs were not sticking out over his lower lip.

"Did you bring bread? Cheese? I've been eating stuff out of the freezer. I don't know what."

"I'll go get some."

"Any gallery would want that. No one will see it ever unless I can break the wall in pieces and re-assemble it."

"Copy it."

"Ignorant girl! No copy is ever as good as the original. That wall has me in it. The essence of my art. The stuff I want to express about the world we live in. I've trapped it there. In that one room. It will never be seen. Except by a few."

"Not everybody would like it."

"Like! What the fuck has like got to do with it? Haven't you learnt anything! Go away and paint pretty scenes. Paint calendars for nice old ladies. Cards for Valentine's Day. Get out."

"I'll take my paints and stuff."

"Goodbye."

She went out to the studio and sat for a moment on the stool beside the easel he allowed her to use. The darkness in the man's mind, in anyone's mind, was his own affair. As long as it didn't spill over into life. She went to the canvasses leaning up against the wall and tipped them forward. It was the first time she'd been in the studio alone. Once again, she was betraying the confidence he placed in her. There were five pictures of her, lying, sitting, standing. He hadn't waited for her to take her clothes off but had imagined her naked body and improved on reality. Her breasts were not as round as that, nor her thighs. And why had he not asked her simply to pose?

She had to leave her paintings and gear there. How could she explain why she wasn't going to see John any more without her mother saying, I told you so? Her Dad wouldn't be surprised.

***

She walked home the long way round, passing houses with the drapes drawn back, the windows clean and open. But what went on in those rooms? Was there any decent life? She wasn't naïve. She was aware of evil. You only had to read the newspapers, watch TV, go to the movies, to know that depravity existed in every imaginable form. But those were other people, other places. As far as she knew John had not committed murder or rape. He had merely expressed himself. *As far as she knew.*

She stopped at the corner store to buy chocolate for herself and a copy of *People* for her mother. As she set the magazine down on the counter, she was struck by the colours on the back cover. Blue sky, blue shirt on the man in the picture, blue shells, blue shadows; all of it advertising a grey-blue car.

The sky was clouding over but between the clouds there was a shade of blue that would have been too pale for Matisse. It was fading to white, to grey, threatening a cold Spring rain. Andrea went back into the store and bought bread and the cheddar cheese John liked. There was the living room to dust and sweep. The painting she'd begun last week, the one with 'real promise', needed more work. And she still had much to learn.

Dear Mr. Sharif

Dear Mr. Sharif,

I read a piece about you in the paper this morning, an interview in which you said you'd given up drink and women and that you are leading a quiet life. I want you to know how glad I am. I feel we have known each other for forty years, ever since I first saw you tramping through the snow to be with your love. You were a modest hero then and I'm pleased that in your old age you have opted for dignity. I didn't want to see you going off debauched into that good night.

We are about the same age but my life has been very different from yours. I mean, for instance, you live free in a fancy hotel in Paris while I live in this little house where I can't really afford to have the bathroom fixed or new tiles laid on the roof. But different or not, we have been tied together with a thread that may be invisible to you but is there all the same. I've always been able to see from your eyes that we are on the same wavelength, so to speak.

So there you were, tramping through the snow in your shabby coat while I was doing exactly the same here in Calgary. Our climates were similar. Our destinations were different. I was going every day to the office where I worked for Mr. Big Oil, and you were going about the world being a star and smiling and suffering across a million cinema screens.

You first became truly exotic to me when I saw you in the desert. Deserts are rare here though I believe there is a small one in British Columbia – without the camels. But there you were all in white, and with that headdress; a sheikh to your toenails. If I'd been there, I would have leapt – can you leap onto a camel? – on to the saddle with you. It would have been easier perhaps if you'd made it kneel down the way they do. In your tent, we would have drunk coffee out of tiny cups and eaten delicate sweet cakes and succulent dates, the sort we used to have at Christmas that came in those oval-shaped boxes. And then as the sun set suddenly as I believe it does in the Sahara because there are no trees or hills for it to sink slowly behind, we might have lain down on your couch.

My husband, gone now these six years, was not great in bed. Sex of the joyful kind was of little interest to him. So you won't mind me telling you that our relationship has been more intimate than you might have imagined. I haven't mentioned your accent in case you are embarrassed about it but I love it; it has always made my heart flutter.

I was sorry a few years ago when I learned that you were spending all your nights playing bridge or hanging around in casinos. It cooled our friendship for a while. Though I suppose you might have said the same thing about me watching the same movie over and over or staying up nights knitting sweaters for the grandkids. Who, by the way, hardly ever come to see me now. I gather that you get to spend time with your grandsons and I'm happy for you.

I'd like to tell you something about the room I'm sitting in as I write this. The two armchairs which face out to the street are covered in blue leather and are extremely comfortable. The table I'm sitting at is marked with stains from hot coffee cups. My late husband had no use for coasters. There is a picture of a sandy beach on the wall and two brass candlesticks on the mantel. Six family photographs stand on top of the television: pictures of our kids when they were little and now their kids, Jeffy and Tanis.

I wonder whose photographs you keep in your hotel room in Paris? I imagine there to be several large pieces of black and white furniture with acres of space between. Someone makes sure there are always fresh flowers. There are fine oriental rugs on the floor. And it smells ever so slightly of incense.

On my bedroom wall there is a picture of you, a poster really, from the movie. It's you dressed in your uniform, looking bewildered and somehow lost. (I called my last cat Zhivago, by the way.) The poster is curling with age and keeps slipping off the wall. Zhivago drowned in the pond when the ice was thin last spring. My neighbour says he can get me a new poster by ordering it on the Internet. I just feel that's very impersonal.

So I have a request, no, not for money, Mr. Sharif, though, being rich, I expect you get a lot of letters asking for help with granny's expenses in the Home or to finance an amateur movie or to send young Dwayne to India to find his soul. Money would spoil what you and I have between us.

Mr. Sharif, though if you'll pardon the liberty I've always called you Omar in private, what I would really like is a photograph, a black and white picture of you as you are now. I don't want one of you as you were then. In a sense we have grown old together and I would like a picture that reflects our age.

I've been too shy to ask before but like you said in the interview, life is for living, not for wasting time.

In return, I'm sending you a picture of myself taken at the company's Christmas dance four years ago. That was the year I retired. The dress isn't something I would ever wear to have dinner with you in your Paris hotel but it was right for that particular occasion.

Well I won't take up any more of your time.

Thank you very much for all the pleasure you have given me over the years and, in advance, for the picture.

Yours most sincerely,
Dorothy.

The Woman Who Drowned in Lake Geneva

"You're going there now?"

"Yes."

"You're meeting someone."

"Don't be ridiculous."

"What'll I do?"

"Go to the Louvre."

Isabel realized that she'd told Jake to go to the Louvre in a tone that implied, Go jump in the Seine. Tired from the long flight, she was trying unobtrusively to change into the outfit she'd brought specially for this day. The uncreasable silk jacket, grey slacks, white blouse with faded pink stain from mother's kiss. She closed the suitcase and looked at herself in the mirror on the back of the door. Unslept, her hair hanging down either side of her face and without makeup, she was plain. A tired, plain woman too impatient to put off this long-planned visit till tomorrow. Jake responded to her suggestion by lying on the bed and turning his face to the wall. She'd persuaded him to come to France by giving him some of her frequent flyer points, finding a cheap hotel and promising him Versailles, romance and fine food. As she closed the door, she heard him say, "Don't be long." Or had he said, "Don't belong?" In any case, it was too late for that warning. And too late to wish that she'd been less generous and had made the trip from Toronto on her own.

She'd traced the route many times in her mind and could have found the building blindfold. Her imaginary walks had always been blest with sunshine, but here in reality rain was dripping down her jacket and splashing up onto her shoes. She stopped a taxi, pronounced the address in the way she'd practised, and looked out of the window to see the well-known shapes of Paris. But the thin triangle of the Tower, the hollowed oblong of the Arch, and the spires of Notre Dame were all hidden by a curtain of mist.

When they reached the house, she handed over too many euros and the driver pulled away while she was trying to remember the word for 'change'. She didn't care. She was here, no longer tired, at the shrine. Standing in front of a stone building in a street busy with twenty-first century traffic. The small gallery on the corner displaying ceramic objects in vivid colours wasn't there in his lifetime. She went through the open front door and turned left. At the entrance to the apartment, a bushy-haired woman sitting beside a table handed out leaflets and accepted donations.

"Bonjour, Madame," she said. Stopping only to nod politely and take a leaflet, Isabel walked on by. She wanted no information, no instructions. She slipped off her raincoat and folded it over her arm. Slowly and with reverence, she entered the study. Perched on a high stool by the window, dominating the room, was the marble bust of the man himself, head resting on his hand, deep in thought – or despair. In his face all the signs of his humanity, his sorrow at being childless, his generosity, his fidelity to Marguerite who was his only love. There was a door in the corner – Isabel had forgotten about the door – and in front of it the armchair covered with an intricate tapestry. Woven into the pattern in soft shades of pink and blue were two angels, one playing a harp and the other waving a tambourine or cymbal. In the photographs, those angels were a mere shady design. Now she was seeing them clear. His desk was the size of a picnic table, bigger than she'd expected. And all that remained on it of the man and his work was a glass inkstand and the well- known lamp, a candelabrum converted to electricity.

On either side of the fireplace hung the controversial pictures: two severe-looking people, a man and a woman in black and white. They were not his parents, and the accepted identity was that of a beloved aunt and uncle. Cynics said he'd bought the pictures from a secondhand store to add a touch of respectable history to his life. The walls were washed in green, a green as pale as snowdrop leaves. Isabel inhaled: Pears. Sorrow. Passion. Vinegar. She glanced at the leaflet the doorkeeper had given her. A marked diagram showed the way to the living room, the bedroom, the kitchen, the maid's room, all of the apartment open to public view. She pushed the paper into her pocket. She was in the only room that mattered, in front of her on the mantelpiece the five figurines she'd travelled three thousand miles to see.

In essays and biographies, they were described as objects of inspiration. From the centre, the rampant lion, one paw on a rock, stared at her hungrily. On either side of the lion, in marble, never destined to connect, stood the nymph and satyr. Smaller than the lion, about nine inches high, they were delicate examples of nineteenth-century sculpture, sculptor unknown. Completing the quintet were the bronze heads of the children. Their faces not angelic. Their sex indeterminate. Both had hyacinth haircuts. The one on the left had a slight sly smile and wide eyes. The other, more serious, had narrow seeker's eyes and a sharp nose. As she looked, the sly one seemed to wink at her, to draw her towards him as if he could tell her a tale or two. Since she'd first seen pictures of them, Isabel had felt that they were non-identical twins, children perhaps of friends. Non-believers said that, like the portraits, they'd been picked up in a flea market to populate the writer's life. In the apartment above, someone was playing the piano. The notes, repeated in an offbeat sequence, built an enticing, labyrinthine melody. He would not have liked it.

In the hotel beside Lake Geneva, waiters carried a harpsichord out onto the lawn and the two young lovers were serenaded by Schubert lieder. Two days later, the bridegroom was listening to a string quartet playing Schumann when the dripping body was brought into the foyer.

Her feelings about the writer were incomprehensible to Jake: You know all there is to know. To Alice: You won't find anything new. To her mother: But you have his books, dear. That a writer, dead for many decades, could fill her with such desire and set her on this pilgrimage made them think her slightly mad. It was normal to make a trip to Graceland or to worship men who pushed a rubber disk across ice with sticks, but pursuit of a dead writer made no sense to them at all. What would they think, Alice, mother, Jake, if they could hear her heart pounding and see her eyes filled with tears? And how could she explain to them that the man who had inhabited this room, written his great prose at that table, was a truly good man. A man who had devoted himself to one beloved woman all his life.

It was the wedding night. In the hotel bedroom, the husband looked out the window, his reluctant bride was slowly taking off her beautiful dress, ivory silk with violets embroidered round the neck and hem, and he saw the figure on the lawn below. A girl in a long white gown looking up at him . . .

In all of his story-telling, the lives the writer portrayed were set against the background of a decadent society, a society which often destroyed the good and poisoned or trapped the weak and unwary. It was a world of lush velvet, of long nights at the theatre, of women and politicians bought and sold, of desperate poverty. But the writer himself gave money to hungry artists and, like his mentor Zola, was reviled for supporting the prisoner of Devil's Island.

Isabel wasn't sure how long she'd been in the room when she heard the voice.

"Excusez-moi." It was a man's voice, an accent she couldn't place.

"I'm sorry."

She moved back to allow the speaker to approach the mantel. The interloper was wearing a damp green jacket and grey slacks and hadn't bothered to take off his hat in homage. In a moment, he'd ruin her visit by turning to her and saying, Lovely, aren't they, or something equally banal. At any rate, he'd broken the spell. Her mind opened to random thoughts: Had Jake roused himself and gone to a museum or was he drowned in sleep? Where would they have dinner? Would her French be good enough to order anything other than an omelette? What would she buy to take back for Alice? For her mother? She shook her head to shoo the images away and concentrated on willing the stranger to leave.

She stared at the back of his head. Grey-black hair showed below his hat. His shoulders hunched forward as if he might reach out and steal the nymph or the lion. If that was his intention, she was ready to jump at him, strike a blow to his upper arm. And if, at that moment, he happened to be holding one of the figurines, it would fall and break into pieces. Then he would blame her, and readers and scholars from all over the world would fire off abusive e-mails to her, some containing death threats, and Jake would say, I told you so.

The bride in her night attire, a shawl over her shoulders, joined her husband at the window. She had come to look out at the romantic moon and to delay the moment when he would lift her onto the bed like a lamb onto the altar. Daringly, she put her hand on his arm . . .

Nothing she'd read since that novel had given Isabel such a thrill of recognition, a feeling of knowing the writer, of being intimate with him. He'd taken words and expanded them, inhaled them and added oxygen so that they meant more than before and were new. She'd sought out his four novels and two novellas and read them slowly over a winter, not wanting to come to the end of his world. She re-read them often. His characters walked and talked with her just as Snow White and Goldilocks had done when she was a child.

For a time, she'd held back from reading *Letters to Marguerite,* published just last year, in case they showed a side of him she'd rather not know. But the letters only confirmed the man to be as admirable in his private life, constant and true in sickness and in health, as in his writing. She only regretted that the lovers' correspondence was now in the public domain, open to every prurient, prying snoop. Laid out there on those pages was his devotion to his wife, to his country and his art. He was not one of those writers who felt that the wild life, drink and women and cruel eccentricities, was the path to literary greatness.

If at any time, I should seem to be a false friend to you, he'd written to his beloved from exile in England, then my blood will turn to water and all my books to ash.

More than one critic had pointed out that this was an empty promise since blood rarely turns to water and, by the time he'd written those words, his books were translated into several languages. There were thousands of copies all over the world, and pandemic spontaneous combustion was unheard of to date. Isabel dismissed such comments as literary spite.

The lake was in one of its calm moods that day. From the hotel came the sound of light laughter and music and when the waiter brought in breakfast, the young bride knew that her life had changed forever. The women promenading below the balcony in their fine gowns, in gold and green and black . . .

The stranger turned towards her, looking at the desk between them, at the inkstand, the lamp. Determined to wait him out, Isabel moved away, inventing a mind-shield, an invisible umbrella that would deflect intrusive and silly comments. She had patented it in sixteen countries by the time he said, "I suppose you're looking for his soul."

"I've always liked his work," she replied, wincing at her own banality.

The man turned to look at the figures on the mantel again. So that was that. He wouldn't annoy her and she could enjoy the atmosphere and ignore him.

Then he said, "Look at the door behind the chair."

The door was dark green, its panels outlined in gold. The tapestry chair stood in front of it like a sentinel; passage interdit, tourists keep out. Even the dead have secrets.

The real guardian, the woman with bushy grey hair who might have been the writer's granddaughter but who was in fact a government employee, came and stood in the hall, not speaking but reminding them that she had to close up, had to get home and cook supper for an ailing husband perhaps or take over the care of her grandchildren so that her daughter, a single mother, could go to her job at the hospital.

Three visitors who had lingered in the other rooms were beginning to make their way out. The old woman barely acknowledged their tips and continued to keep her eye on the two in the study. Isabel looked at her watch. In Toronto it was late morning. Here, it would soon be getting dark. Had she really been awake for a day and a night? Feeling dizzy, she closed her eyes for a moment and opened them to see the man murmuring to the guardian. He slipped a note into her hand, and she retreated. A bribe perhaps.

Ha! A conspiracy. A mystery novel. Chapter Seven: In which our heroine is locked in the writer's house alone and left to confront his ghost. Forced to spend the night on his bed or sit in his chair since she was so keen, so eager to know his life. His shade would appear after midnight and demand to know why she was bothering him, why people couldn't leave him alone. *I am dead for Chrissake!* He would stand there in the corner, point his finger like old Marley and say, *Read my works.* She shivered and decided to leave.

But then the disturbing man said, "None of this furniture was his."

"Yes it was," Isabel retorted.

"No it wasn't."

"How do you know? Who are you?"

He took off his hat and said, "Look at my face."

She looked and saw the sly smile of the child on the left, and the eyes and forehead from the picture on a million dustjackets.

"He had no children."

"My great-grandfather had two children. And you won't find his soul here or anywhere else. You look pale. Sit down."

He removed the card that warned visitors to keep off, and Isabel sat on the tapestry chair and leaned back against the angels. She felt a little faint and a little afraid. It was a fear now not of the dead but the living. Fear is the enemy of love. The writer had put those words, not entirely original, into the mouth of the young husband as he was removing his bride's shoes and seeing her feet for the first time.

"I come here once a month," the man said, "and usually I don't talk to anyone, but I saw you standing there and I knew you were one of the serious ones. Not someone who only wants to go home and say, I saw where he wrote, I touched his table, I sat in his chair."

"He's meant a great deal to me."

"You're a teacher?"

"Just an admirer."

She wasn't about to explain to a stranger that she'd stopped teaching because the students had given up any traditional approach to math and spoke a language she couldn't understand. Or that she found her work in the Statistics Department satisfying and . . . it was none of his business.

"Whose furniture is it?"

"He never sat at that desk."

"Where then?"

"When Marguerite discovered he was seeing a woman half her age, she made a bonfire of all his favourite furniture. Out there in the garden. The shock brought on his death. That and the German army on the outskirts of the city."

"That's not true. You've made it all up."

"There was time between his death and hers, eleven years, for her to create a myth."

She looked at his face again. It was easy to smile slyly and to brush your hair forward and claim a relationship.

"And what about the lion, the children?"

"Where were you when you first read *The Woman Who Drowned in Lake Geneva?*"

In Hell. Sitting under a maple tree. Sunlight filtering through the leaves, speckling the pages. My boyfriend had told me I was too possessive. My Pure Math professor had made an impure suggestion. I could hardly make out the words on the page for tears.

"At university," she said.

"It changed your life?"

"Not my life." She wasn't going to allow him that. "It changed my ideas of life, my, my approach to life – at that moment."

"Ah. Well then, I'll be off."

"What about the door? What's behind it?"

"Evidence."

So he wanted to show her some secret that would take away the magic of years, a world she had happily inhabited. How much did truth matter? The writer himself had said more than once that truth was beyond price. Also that some doors were best kept closed.

"Who do you think the woman who drowned in Lake Geneva was?"

"It was fiction."

"This furniture is fiction."

He took a key from his pocket, a loose key, not one on a ring with others, and turned it in the lock of the green door. She stood up, not wanting to look. Were there bodies? Real skeletons? Was he about to drag her inside and attack her? Was the old woman a pimp? Would anyone hear if she yelled, 'M'aidez!'

When he moved to one side to let her see into the dark space, Isabel backed away so that he couldn't push her in and leave her there. She glanced towards the inside of the closet. As her eyes adjusted to the shadows, she cried out. There was someone in there. A tall woman draped in white leaning against the wall. "Go on. Touch!"

He lifted the sheet and pushed her towards the figure. Isabel put her fingers on the yellowed, disintegrating gown. That's all it was, a gown. It was the gown! The ivory wedding dress with violets round the neck and hem. She'd planned to wear a copy of it if she ever married. On a hook above hung the lacy hat with the remains of two silk roses on the worn brim. Beneath the dress, the shoes, the two-strap button-over shoes which the husband had unfastened so slowly on the first night of the honeymoon.

"Marguerite's wedding clothes," the man said.

Isabel wanted to run down the hall and into the street and shout that she had been betrayed. *Who by, my love?* A dead author! She wanted to accuse this man of faking the whole thing. Did he expect her now to be so overcome that she'd fall into his arms and go for a glass of wine with him? Go to bed with him? Validate Jake's accusation that she was meeting someone?

"Jerome Serain at your service."

Common sense returned.

"Why haven't you told about this? Gone public with it?"

"A man's ghost is sometimes stronger than truth."

"What's to stop me telling the world?"

"Do you want to?"

No, she did not. Oh, the gasping delight of his critics, of the scholars who would open new doors to speculation and iconoclastic delight. And a horde of people who cared nothing for the book would come to finger the gown till it was nothing but scraps. She backed out of the closet and sat again on the chair.

"And the woman who drowned in Lake Geneva?"

"His first mistress. In despair because he'd married Marguerite, she followed them to the hotel. She was only nineteen."

"The children?"

"Hers. Three months old. She left a note, asking him to care for them. He never acknowledged them. Never spoke about that night or the infants. Marguerite found out years later. For the twins it meant orphanages, poverty, deprivation. There was no place for them in his life. His art came first."

Jerome Serain closed the door of the sad closet, locked it and put the key back in his pocket. The room became dark. The custodian had dimmed the lights from a remote switch. Their time was up. Isabel glanced round. In the shadows, the figurines, the pictures, the table were just so many commonplace objects in the room of an ordinary man.

"Why did you tell me this?"

"Secrets can get heavy."

"What do you do?"

"Just say I'm a writer who shows some promise."

"Your accent?"

"I grew up in Wales. I live here now. Would you like to come for a glass of wine?"

"My lover is waiting for me in the hotel," she said.

"They usually are," he replied.

Isabel asked if the other books were also based on the great man's life.

"No, only that one story – it's always only one story."

She stepped out of the building. The rain had stopped. A line of poetry came into her head. *Love is not love which alters when it alteration finds.* She couldn't recall the rest; she only knew that it was from a Shakespeare sonnet and that it was true. She smiled and turned back to Jerome and told him that, after all, she did have time for a glass of wine.

Scenes from Her Life

LORRAINE LAY IN THE OPEN COFFIN stripped of all knowledge, free from facts. The customary defiant look was gone and only a slight accepting smile was left on her lips. Tomorrow others would come to view the woman who hadn't been easy to like. Worth making the effort to know her, her two friends said and they at least would cry. Guilt would bring others to the chapel to murmur pieties and inhale the scent of funereal lilies. *If we'd been kinder, could she have been saved?*

Sam hadn't spoken to his sister since the quarrel at Dad's funeral two years ago. And it wasn't a fight over money; there'd been none to speak of. The *casus belli* was a simple figurine the old man had bought on one of his 'eco-tourism' trips to Africa. He claimed it was a centuries-old idol from a secluded tribe. Eco-tourism was a concept the old man hadn't quite grasped. He'd thought snapping pictures of giraffes from a jeep, watching lions kill their prey, going to sea on a Japanese whaling vessel brought him closer to nature – until Lorraine made him talk to the man from the Sierra Club. It was a matter, she said, of setting him right. She could never resist that, setting people right. Like the neurologist at her friend's dinner party. She'd argued with him about the best approach to brain surgery, losing both friend and the chance of boasting that she knew the top doctor in the field.

The day of dividing up the spoils at 23 Powell Court hadn't even begun amicably. All three of them were there, Lorraine,

Jane and himself. I thought you were going to clean the place. I didn't hear you offering to help. Empty of its spirit, the house seemed small and mean. Books and papers and piles of photographs were lying around as if the old man had been trying to make sense of his life in those last days. And the little statue, eighteen inches high, clay-coloured, gaping mouth, closed eyes, smudge of a nose, was standing on the coffee table. It did, Sam thought, have some kind of drawing power and for a moment they all sat there looking at it.

***

[*At an unheard signal both women make a grab for the little relic.*]

LORRAINE: He meant me to have this.

JANE: He said it was mine every time I came to see him.

LORRAINE: And just how often was that?

JANE: He thought you were bossy.

LORRAINE: He said you were lazy.

[*They both pull and the figurine breaks in half leaving some of its ancient dust on the table.*]

LORRAINE AND JANE IN UNISON: Look what you've done now.

LORRAINE [*takes a deep breath and heads for the moral high ground*]: You and Sam are just like him. You do what you do without thinking of the consequences. I was planning to give this to a museum and now look at it. It was worth thousands of dollars.

[*She throws her half onto the floor and it crumbles into fragments.*]

JANE: You bitch. It could have been glued.

LORRAINE [*looks at Sam*]: Worthless!

[*She walks quietly out of the house picking up on her way their father's other prized possession, an illegally bought narwhal tusk from Nunavut.*]

***

Sam can see her now going out holding the ivory trophy to her side like a general on parade, and Jane following her down the path shouting, "He was my father too," for all the neighbours to hear.

Jane was letting her tears drop on to the suit Lorraine's corpse was wearing.

"She wanted perfection. That was all. She often meant to be kind. Like the time – like the time she insisted on driving me to the airport. I knew it was terminal 1. She told me it was terminal 3. She knew. She was sure. She was wrong. I missed the flight. But she had meant to be kind, I guess."

Lorraine's kindness had a sort of built-in cruelty, Sam thought, and as he looked into the casket, he tried to stifle bitterness. She'd never accepted that his was a valid occupation and that last suggestion of hers was downright insulting. It was a Wednesday. He knew that because it was the day he took off each week to do the chores, the shopping, and answer mail. And it was Jess's last day of vacation. A warm September day.

***

[*In the kitchen of his one-bedroom apartment.*]

JESS: The wicked witch of the East is coming?

SAM: She's your aunt. Be nice.

JESS: She'll tell me I'm taking the wrong courses again.

[*The intercom beeps.*]

SAM: Come up.

[*He puts dirty dishes in the sink. Throws grubby towel into drawer. Lorraine enters.*]

LORRAINE: I know it's your day. You still here, Jess? Shouldn't you be at your mother's?

[*Jess is silent.*]

LORRAINE: I want to talk to your Dad.

[*Jess is silent.*]

SAM: That's OK.

LORRAINE: If you say so. I'm on my way to a meeting. I just stopped in to say, Sam, that I know a man at PeriVision. It would mean spending a while doing re-writes but you'd be earning more and it's a foot in the door. Commercials are very lucrative. I mean what did your last little effort bring in? Did anyone come to see it after that awful review? I felt badly for you. The way he even blamed you for the scenery.

[*Jess leaves the kitchen.*]

[*Sam says thank you. After some offhand chat about the family and the weather, Lorraine hands him a card and leaves. Jess returns.*]

JESS: She didn't stay long.

SAM: I guess she has 'calls of a similar nature to make.' [*Both laugh.*]

***

Jess had made coffee then and stroked his ego by telling him that last play was his best and the critics were only into grandstanding and before long, he would be recognised. But he was forty-five and the world wasn't beating a path. Artistic directors answered his calls – eventually. His agent had a high degree of hope. What did Lorraine know about the excitement of live theatre, the thrill of taking risks, the shiver of fear in that dark moment before the stage lights go up?

But it was a different scene that made Sam want to shake his sister back to life and ask her what the hell she'd meant. Place: the other kitchen. Time: earlier on the same day as the shattering of the little statue. He'd been staying in their father's house, sorting out bills and mail, tidying around so they could put the property on the market. And Lorraine swishing in, wearing a silky green outfit that must have cost a thousand or two, had said, "Hand in the cookie jar like always?"

He'd been about to ask what she was talking about when Jane arrived in a kind of hysterical fog and they had to calm her down. And then, after the figurine incident, there'd been no more conversation. Except that she'd said *worthless* right into his face.

He recalled some distinguished speaker at a graduation ceremony re-hashing the old line about this not being an end but a beginning. And this now was the beginning of life without Lorraine, on whom they'd depended for that kind of aggravation that either creates pearls in oyster shells or remains as constant irritation. There'd been no apparent residual jewels in her case.

Jane said, "When I was about ten she told me they'd christened me Jane because they knew I'd be plain."

"You're not plain," he said as sincerely as he could.

Beside the well-dressed woman in the casket he felt shabby. His suit was years old. Maybe she'd been right about him not being a great father. If he'd been more attentive, Jess might not have had so many parts of her body pierced or gone in for that unsightly tattoo. But how could you stop kids these days? True, if she'd gone somewhere more sanitary she might not have lost that small piece from her earlobe.

Jane reached for his hand and said, "I wish I'd talked back to her more. She used to shout me down. Not that she shouted but there was the force of it. You couldn't ever win."

Jane was wearing one of Lorraine's old outfits. It was too tight round her breasts and a little long in the waist. Sam wondered how she could have had the nerve to raid her sister's wardrobe quite so soon. But Jane said Lorraine was nothing if not practical and wouldn't have wanted her good clothes to go to waste. Something had 'gone to waste' here but Sam wasn't at all sure what it was. He felt guilty about wanting to get home in time for the start of the game. He needed to sit in front of the TV with a beer and lose himself in action. Death was too static.

"Jess coming tomorrow?" Jane asked.

"No," he said.

Jess wouldn't forgive Lorraine for the loss of Larry Roskov. It wasn't interference, Lorraine had said when Sam confronted her, it was making sure. She'd checked up on the kid, a kid of eighteen, discovered that his Dad was a little on the dishonest side and made a pronouncement about apples not falling far from the tree. Of course the boy had found out and blamed Jess for spying on his family, yelled at her for being a snob and walked away. Jess had gone to her aunt and told her to mind her own business. After that, she built a romantic fantasy around Larry as the man she might have loved forever. She had, though, loved three others since.

Jane said, "You have to forgive and forget. Jess will learn that. I've done a lot of it lately."

He looked at his 'little' sister. She was small and lived a small life, but since the separation was making an effort to move on. She came to his plays and told him she heard people say good things in the intermission. She talked of taking a course in ancient pottery at the university and saving up to go to Erzerum. She didn't often speak out but when she did, the sky fell.

★★★

Thanksgiving 2001

Lorraine and Michel greeted them at the door of their townhouse. Michel looked like a man with vine leaves in his hair. Perhaps they'd just had sex though Sam couldn't, didn't want to, imagine that for Chrissake.

"Come in," Lorraine says to the three of them, to him and Jess and Diane.

> [*Michel pours wine for them. Offers them a cocktail but is stopped by Lorraine who says hard liquor will affect their taste buds and she hasn't spent two days in the kitchen for nothing. If they want cocktails let them go eat at McDonalds. There is warm family feeling all round. Enter Jane and Don.*]

DON: Cold out there.

> [*Random chat till Lorraine calls them to come into the dining room.*]

A fluffy feathered turkey stands in the centre of the table with candles around it. Immaculate place settings. Linen napkins in little silver turkey holders of all the crazy things. Dinner is ready and the women help Lorraine to carry in tureens of vegetables and gravy in a bowl. Michel brings in the turkey he has cooked.

Michel carves the turkey.

Everyone is served. Everyone is polite.

Have you got peas? More gravy?

The salad will be handed round after the main course.

Jane says, "Cranberry sauce?"

Lorraine puts down her knife and fork.

"Did I forget something?" she asks.

"It's all right," Jane says.

"Jam with meat is passé," Diane puts in.

"Michel," Lorraine says. "The corner store is still open. Could you run down and get a can of cranberry jelly for my sister."

Michel answers, "No."

"Well I will."

[*Lorraine gets up and leaves. They hear the car start.*]

Don yells at Jane and digs up a decade of disagreements to follow his, "See what you've done."

"Eat it while it's hot," Michel says.

Lorraine did return but not till the food was cold on the table and they were all in the kitchen trying to make it as tidy as they could without speaking to one another.

Christmas 1969

Dad had done his best with the tree. He liked to decorate it himself. Mom the gift-giver was handing out the presents. Jane aged six kept on chattering about how wonderful it was that Santa managed to get into an apartment with no chimney. Sam aged nine kept quiet. And then Lorraine said Jane was old enough to know that Santa was a story and Mom and Dad bought the presents and she should be grateful to them. Dad hauled Lorraine out of the room and Sam could still hear the slap and the outraged yell and see the smirk on little Jane's face.

***

The solemn man was coughing as if they were wasting his time by lingering so long in his chapel of rest. There were other bodies, other bereaved family members waiting for him.

Jane said, "She did help when Don left me. She did. Although she said I should have made more of an effort."

Were they missing something? Lorraine had tried. *She* had made an effort.

He looked at Jane and knew they were not a convincing pair. Not people you'd immediately look to in difficult times, whereas Lorraine in spite of her nature was a rock.

"Did she feel unloved?" he asked, almost understanding her in that moment.

The attendant said, "Would you prefer the casket closed or open?"

"What about Michel?" Jane whispered.

"He's not here."

Sam took a last look at his dead sister, the oldest, the responsible one, the one who worked six days a week, sat on several volunteer committees and tried to save her small part of the world. She had thought him ineffectual; he should have been more ambitious, supported his ex-wife, saved more for Jess's education. *I'm doing my best, Lorraine, working as hard as I can.* He needed time out to pick up ideas, to listen to dialogue in bars, in coffee shops. Picking up local colour was part of his trade, just as going to conferences and seeking better inventions had been part of hers.

But he knew as he looked down at her that she had to some extent been right about him.

"Close the damn casket," he said.

And waited till he got home to cry.

II

The shell was perfect, pink and oyster-coloured. They'd picked it up on their honeymoon as they walked along that sandy beach in Florida where every incoming tide washed treasures ashore. Lorraine had admired the symmetry of the pale shell's concentric curves and said, "It really makes you want to believe in God." It was an amazing piece of engineering, a perfect thing, and Michel had loved her for loving it. He put it in his pocket to take to the funeral home.

He looked round the place that had been home to him for twelve years. There was nothing of his in the house now except a few books and some CDs he always planned to pick up and never had. We'll stay friends, she'd said when he moved out. And he had let her down in that way too. She who never let anyone down, to whom a promise was sacred. *Why are you doing that? Because I said I would.*

"I'm sorry, Lorraine," he said.

He'd tried to shorten her name, calling her Lorry or even Rainy but she hated both.

And three days ago, she'd lain here on the floor, unable to get help, perhaps calling his name, and died alone. He felt afraid. The life of a vigorous woman had been so soon extinguished. How long before it was his turn, before he was cold and forgotten? The nuns had taught him to look forward to an afterlife but he had lost his place there years ago.

He picked up the photograph she loved: the two of them with the former Prime Minister. True she was a snob but her ability to reach out to the 'right' people had helped his career as well as raising money for her pet project. If she liked to drop the names of the VIPs she met, it was a harmless pleasure.

He dreaded the next few hours. Even the wreaths would murmur *hypocrite* when he walked into the chapel. All the mourners would silently insult his tears. They would think, he knew they would, that for him it had been a merciful release: he would be free now, free of her nagging calls, her slighting remarks. They would, among themselves, in whispers, suggest that he had killed her by neglect. He was about to walk into a cloud of misunderstanding. He found her stand-by bottle of

Napoleon and poured a shot into a mug. *The brandy glasses are over there, Michel.*

He'd deliberately kept away from the funeral home the day before although he obviously had rights. Let her siblings do what they wanted, he'd thought, but all the same he didn't want to be a guest at his ex-wife's obsequies. Had they still been together, he would have arranged it himself in every detail, aware that she was looking over his shoulder. The candles and the flowers would have been exactly what she liked and there would be no lilies.

It was almost time to face the music. The music! No doubt Sam and Jane had chosen something entirely predictable like 'Air on a G string' 'Abide with me' or, worst of all, 'Amazing Grace.' Lorraine was not always into grace and if she'd had time to write out the details of the ceremony, would have specified a kilted man playing a rousing march on the bagpipes, a reflection of their Scottish ancestry. She always hinted at a castle and servants but Sam said their grandfather had been a gamekeeper, and wouldn't allow that the family had any right to a particular tartan though Lorraine said that every Scotsman was descended from one clan or another. And she was probably, as nearly always, right.

They'd remained at odds with her, her siblings. Though Don, Jane's ex, and Diane, Sam's ex, were quite friendly as if that awful Thanksgiving Dinner had been specially arranged to release them from their mates.

The trouble had begun when Jane, in that meek malevolent way she had, said, "You've forgotten the cranberry sauce." She was always pleased to have a chance to correct her superior sister. "What's turkey without cranberry sauce?" she went on and her husband, Don, gave her a shove that nearly knocked her off her chair.

Fat Diane had jumped in with a word about jam for heaven's sake and Sam had told her she was stupid and should shut up.

And Diane had responded that since she kept their family going perhaps he was the one who should hold his tongue.

Michel could see that Lorraine was steaming. She'd been planning the dinner for weeks and had set everything out the night before. They'd been up till midnight measuring the table in order to place the ornamental turkey in the exact centre of it.

"There's no need for cranberry sauce," he'd said in response to Jane. "We have everything here we need."

And that was when Lorraine had looked at him and realised from the way he spoke, from his voice, that he was screwing Sharon. It was his tone of conciliation that let him down. She went away in order to collect herself. None of the others noticed that she brought nothing back with her, they were too busy trying to clean up and leave the place neat to her high standards.

★★★

It would be a mixed group of attendees at the ceremony. Women who knew her only as the volunteer who helped set up their refuge and sought money to keep it going loved her. Her colleagues from the company, from her day job, had feelings that varied from mixed to unequivocal dislike. She got things done but not without scarring some of the men and women lower down the ladder. Perhaps, as at a wedding, ushers might ask, Are you with Saint Lorraine or Bitch Lorraine and guide the mourners to the chairs on the left or the right according to the answer.

Who besides himself had known her as admirable and lovable?

Who had truly appreciated her?

Michel wanted to address the assembly the way people did at funerals nowadays. Too many often wanted to get in a word about the deceased, tell jokes, provoke laughter when tears were more appropriate. *He/she would have wanted you all to have a good time.* Very likely! He/she probably would have preferred tears and wailing and rending of garments. *Let's have a real show of grief here, people.*

His few words, more of a declaration, had run through his mind for the last two nights almost without stopping, edited and re-edited till it was almost a poem.

You think you knew my wife, my ex-wife. You think you knew our marriage, our ex-marriage. I'd like to tell you a few things. Bear with me. You'll be able to get at the wine and sushi and cheese soon enough. Sit still and listen. She is still now but not listening.

If she'd known she was going to die, she would have organised this event down to the food and guest list. She would have cleaned the house, and polished the silver till you could see your faces in it.

I know what you all think. But it wasn't like that. I did kiss Sharon that day because she practically fell into my arms and murmured about me needing someone gentle and kind. Lorraine's appearance in the doorway was an awful mischance. She very rarely came to the office.

***

When he'd first seen Lorraine, she was on a platform in the Queen Elizabeth Hotel in Montreal making a speech about the advance of electronic devices for the handicapped and the need for more research funding, and the guy sitting next to him had said, "I bet she's a ball-breaker."

Michel had been attracted by the determination that showed in the lines of her face, the planes of her cheeks, her regular mouth. He'd seen a portrait in a private collection. The artist had outlined the jaw with a darkish tint and painted the eyebrows square. If he'd had the money, and he might now, he would have tried to buy it.

He'd known at first glance that she wasn't a simple woman, an easy-to-please woman. He found a seat next to her at the afternoon presentation and asked her out for a drink that evening.

"I'm younger than you are," he'd said, giving her a reason to turn him down.

"All the better, you'll care for me when I'm old," she replied, making the assumption that once they'd slept together, they would marry and be each other's for life.

He'd only wanted to get this brilliant woman into bed, to 'own' her at least for that weekend. But she had taken him on. She had embraced him. And her embrace was like that of a giant octopus. She grasped him. She understood him. She improved him.

Never after their wedding had he gone to work in an ill-fitting suit, a rumpled shirt, a badly chosen tie. Never had he gone without a good breakfast and when he took lunch to work with him, it was a good lunch.

The rule became that since he got home first, he made dinner and served her a drink. And that was the comfortable way of their lives. Although comfort was not how it always appeared to others in a house so clean that motes of dust retreated and hardly dared to land on the polished surfaces.

★★★

None of you can understand the kind of nobility she had when she said to me, "Go. You're still young. You'll have children."

"I don't love Sharon," I said to her.

"Has that mattered?" she asked, looking at me with those big eyes.

And I understood then that she hadn't known.

She closed the door on our marriage, put me outside it, made me free. When all I wanted was to get back in.

***

He wanted to tell them that she was capable of poetry. One evening, she'd called him outside to look at the full moon apparently balanced on a power line and although the earth moved and took away the illusion, the enchantment had stayed for a while. She was open to magic.

***

Yes, she called a few days ago and asked me to go round and fix the alarm system and I didn't make it. It wasn't callousness, it was the feeling you have that there will be another day and a day after that. I was busy.

***

He was still rehearsing the words when he arrived at the Home. Its white pillars, perhaps supposed to look like pearly gates, repelled him. There were many cars, many people arriving. He joined her brother and sister and stood by the door as more mourners came in, more, he imagined, than Lorraine knew. In their years together, she'd hardly ever gone out with friends. The music as he feared was the usual canned funeral pap. But then it segued suddenly into something she loved, a fragment of Gorecki's *Symphony of Sorrowful Songs,* as if she'd changed the disc herself.

He felt for the shell in his pocket. It wouldn't pay the boatman for the journey; it was simply a treasure to keep her company.

He went into the chapel where she lay to put it beside her.

"Who closed the damn casket?" he shouted.

Sam started and clutched his heart. Afterwards he said he thought Lorraine had spoken.

Jane apologised. The attendant said he could open it if he must. Michel said it was all right.

They were led to the front row. Don and Diane were sitting across the aisle. Michel, in a whisper, demanded to know why they'd closed the coffin without his permission. Sam the playwright looked like a hollow man and only shook his head. What would he and Jane do now without their big sister to wind them up? The absent Jess was probably still sulking about that young good-for-nothing and might never know that her aunt had loved her.

The music changed again. It was beginning, the tidying away of a proud and remarkable woman. A man in a white robe was talking about the 'farther shore'. Michel lost that voice and instead heard Lorraine talking in that firm way she had about the current scandal. They'd argued about politics, she from the right, he from the centre, and now she was calling his name. He was to go forward and look at the people and say what couldn't be said.

As he stood up, he recalled how she'd looked when she spoke those chilling words, "Has it mattered?"

He turned to the rows of faces and all his thoughts fled. Someone coughed. There was expectation in the room. Finally he said, "My heart is broken," and sat down again. Let them make of that what they would. He could hear gasps behind him, a few murmured words, then silence.

The coffin slid along a conveyor belt and out of sight.

The clergyman was about to say a final prayer when Jane marched forward, urged him to one side and stood behind the lectern. Only her eyes and her hat could be seen over the edge. She appeared to be waving a piece of clay that gave off showers of dust.

"You will all come to this," she said. "Like Lorraine. We weren't good enough for her. She was better than any of you. You are not adequate. What is wrong with trying to be perfect? I'd like to sing this song because when she was a teenager she listened to it all the time. And you will join in now."

Sam was starting towards the podium but Michel stopped him and Jane began to sing slowly, quite in tune, "Take a sad song and make it better."

No one did join in but she went on singing the same line over and over till everyone had left.

III

Jane was sitting in the washroom crying. But this was a funeral and tears were expected. It was a cover for any kind of sorrow, even for weeping with embarrassment. They'd probably thought she was crazy singing like that but she only wanted to fill a gap, a grief-deficiency. There simply wasn't enough emotion in that room. Or rather there'd been a mixture of contrary feelings. Half the people probably didn't much like the deceased. A few of them regarded Michel as a murderer by default. Some of them had admired her and known who she really was. And the two or three who'd been expecting help from her were most likely as much annoyed as sorry that Lorraine was dead.

She washed her face, applied fresh lipstick and went out to join the others, prepared to hear again all the usual phrases. The insensitive: Such an awful way to go. The reproachful: If only someone had stopped by. The useless: She would have been pleased to see so many here.

She couldn't see Michel anywhere. Sam had probably gone ahead to open the door to her house for early arrivals. *All right, Lorraine, so the place isn't polished up to your standards but I tidied up and dusted and washed those glasses that haven't been used since Don left me. The wine is decent and there are platters of cheese and fruit and little cakes covered in wrap.*

There were still a lot of people hanging around. If they all went back, there wouldn't be enough food. She'd only catered for thirty and half that would be a more likely number. Lorraine, had she known she was about to die, would have sent out invitations and expected people to respond.

Jane pulled herself together and walked into the throng. These people had to be thanked for coming. A woman hugged her wordlessly and moved on.

An older woman murmured, "This is a sad time, my dear."

Jane said, "You understood why I sang?"

"I thought it was a recording," the woman replied.

Karaoke at a funeral would be something new!

A sad-looking man detached himself from a group and came towards her.

"You knew her well?" Jane asked.

He nodded.

"She was a great person. Not easy. If you worked with her, then you'd know that. But she got things done and she did have a way of arranging life. Maybe she was a bit interfering and I know she could be downright aggravating."

An elaborate floral arrangement on a nearby table caught her eye. "I'll take those with me. I expect we've paid for them."

The man watched her pick up the vase and stared at her as she went on talking. "But she wanted things to be the best, and people too. So I suppose she was disappointed generally in just about everybody. And that's why in the end, the marriage didn't work. Nobody is perfect though I do think he tried, certainly at first. I'm sorry. I'm going on. It's the shock. How long had you known her?"

"She was my wife."

Jane took a close look at the man. He was not Michel. She glanced round the room. There was no one here that she knew. She was among strangers and suddenly all of them appeared to have animal heads. They were donkeys, bears, wolves, braying and barking.

"Sorry," she said and walked away still clutching the flowers.

"Wait a minute," the husband called after her. "What did you know about our marriage? What did she say to you?"

"I'm in the wrong place. Excuse me."

★★★

She ran outside to her car, the man shouting after her.

Oh dear, she said to Lorraine. I have to do better than this.

The friends and relatives would be wondering where on earth she was. She drove quickly and when she got to the house couldn't understand why there were no cars parked on the street. Had no one at all come back to pay their respects? Then she saw that she was outside Lorraine's house, not her own. *Wrong again, plain Jane.* The police tape was gone. The room had probably been cleaned up. They hadn't caught the man who had come in and bashed Lorraine over the head and taken her computer, her money, and the narwhal tusk. The doctor said she'd been alive for a day and a night after the attack, lying there helpless.

★★★

Jane had never told the others after that awful Thanksgiving Dinner about finding a dish of home-made cranberry sauce in the fridge when she was putting the leftovers away. She'd pushed it to the back, along with the question of why Lorraine had rushed out the way she did.

Later she'd figured it had to do with Michel. Sam had always said that no one would marry Lorraine; she had as much sex appeal as the Statue of Liberty. But Sam wasn't smart about women. Michel and Lorraine had been happy for a while. The funny thing was that three supposedly happily married couples had sat down at that table and a few months later they were all separated – single, for better or for worse.

She put the car into gear and set off towards her own home. Jess had promised to turn up there, to be a dutiful niece, no doubt with her latest disaster in tow. Perhaps now that Lorraine was dead, she'd find herself a decent boyfriend.

★★★

There were about fifty people crammed into the house, leaning against the walls, sitting on the furniture, the floor, in the hall, in the kitchen. She hesitated to look upstairs. Dreamy music, not hers, was playing in the background. Michel was pouring wine as if he really was the bereaved husband. Jess had gone out to get more food from the delicatessen. It was beginning to sound like a party. Was she in the wrong place again? Sam looking worried asked her where she'd been. She didn't answer. Michel kissed her and gave her a glass of Chardonnay.

And there was Don accepting condolences as if he were still part of the family. At least he'd had the decency not to bring his new woman. When he saw Jane he came to give her a hug. "She's probably left you some money," he said.

"It won't be much," Jane answered, promising to herself that he would get none of it nor would he be allowed to know the amount if she could help it. Let him keep on paying that measly amount of alimony till he was old and his hair and teeth fell out, hopefully all at once on the same day.

"I'll miss her too," he said.

Goodbye, Don.

★★★

Michel had told her that indeed Lorraine had left her something. She tried to suppress images of a new bathroom, a modern kitchen. It was too soon to make plans.

She walked round saying to this one and that, yes, it was a terrible loss, and thinking that maybe with the legacy she could quit her job at the store and write a book of suitable and original words to say to the bereaved. *Death for Dummies.*

By five o'clock everyone had gone. Sam had offered to stay with her but she knew he wanted to get back to his computer. Lorraine's awful end had inspired him. He was going to write an intense drama: the thoughts of a woman dying alone as scenes from her life played through her mind.

Michel, still dazed, perhaps truly heart-broken, had tidied the kitchen before he left and even mopped the floor. He told Jane to call him if she needed any help. It was a limited offer. In three weeks' time he was going to move back to Montreal.

She emptied the remains of a bottle of wine into her glass and sat down to think about Turkey, a country that had now become nearer. She undid the buttons of her jacket, Lorraine's elegant black wool jacket, and breathed more easily. Then she saw it. Beside the travel agent's leaflets on the coffee table lay a large pink seashell. It hadn't been there in the morning. She sat back. She wasn't drunk. It looked very like the one Lorraine had kept on her bathroom counter. She picked the shell up and admired its perfect whorls and put it to her ear to listen to the sea. There might be a reasonable explanation for its presence here but she preferred the mystery.

"Thank you, sister," she said and lifted her glass to heaven where Lorraine was very likely arguing with God.

Acknowledgements

I would like to thank Joan Coldwell and Ann Saddlemyer for asking me one day if I happened to have any stories and then for their thoughtful work in producing this collection after I replied, "Funny you should ask."

I am very grateful to Pat Martin Bates for allowing her art to be used on the cover, and to Frances Hunter for the design.

And I bow to the ghost of Nathaniel Hawthorne whose *Tanglewood Tales* were a delightful part of my children's early reading and who is always present in my study.

RACHEL WYATT was born in Bradford, England in 1929; she immigrated to Canada with her family in 1957. From 1986 she taught in the Writing Programme at the Banff Centre for the Arts and was Director of the Programme from 1992 to 2001. For eight years she led a series of writing workshops at Arctic College, Iqaluit, Baffin Island.

A prolific writer of radio drama (over one hundred plays produced by the BBC and CBC), she also writes for live theatre, with plays staged across Canada, in the United States and in Britain.

Wyatt has published six novels and two previous volumes of stories: her collection *The Day Marlene Dietrich Died* (1996) was brought out in Italian by Voland Edizióni, Rome. She is also the author of a biography of Agnes Macphail, first woman elected to the Canadian House of Commons.

Rachel Wyatt is a member of the Order of Canada and recipient of the Queen's Jubilee Medal.

Author photograph by Joan Coldwell